Geoffrey de Villehardouin

Memoirs or Chronicle of The Fourth Crusade and The Conquest of Constantinople

Outlook

Geoffrey de Villehardouin

Memoirs or Chronicle of The Fourth Crusade and The Conquest of Constantinople

1. Auflage | ISBN: 978-3-73262-454-6

Erscheinungsort: Frankfurt am Main, Deutschland

Erscheinungsjahr: 2018

Outlook Verlag GmbH, Frankfurt.

Geoffrey de Villehardouin

Memoirs or Chronicle of The Fourth Crusade and The Conquest of Constantinople

Outlook

Memoirs or Chronicle of The Fourth Crusade and The Conquest of Constantinople

by Geoffrey de Villehardouin

THE FIRST PREACHING OF THE CRUSADE

1

Be it known to you that eleven hundred and ninety-seven years after the Incarnation of our Lord Jesus Christ, in the time of Innocent Pope of Rome, and Philip King of France, and Richard King of England, there was in France a holy man named Fulk of Neuilly - which Neuilly is between Lagni-sur- Marne and Paris - and he was a priest and held the cure of the village. And this said Fulk began to speak of God throughout the Isle-de-France, and the other countries round about; and you must know that by him the Lord wrought many miracles.

Be it known to you further, that the fame of this holy man so spread, that it reached the Pope of Rome, Innocent*; and the Pope sent to France, and ordered the right worthy man to preach the cross (the Crusade) by his authority. And afterwards the Pope sent a cardinal of his, Master Peter of Capua, who himself had taken the cross, to proclaim the Indulgence of which I now tell you, viz., that all who should take the cross and serve in the host for one year, would be de-

[note: Innocent III, elected Pope on the 8th January 1 98, at the early age of thirty seven, Innocent III was one of the leading spirits of his time-in every sense a strong man and great Pope. From the beginning of his pontificate he turned his thoughts and policy to the recovery of Jerusalem.]

2

livered from all the sins they had committed, and acknowledged in confession. And because this indulgence was so great, the hearts of men were much moved, and many took the cross for the greatness of the pardon.

OF THOSE WHO TOOK THE CROSS

The other year after that right worthy man Fulk had so spoken of God, there was held a tourney in Champagne, at a castle called Ecri, and by God's grace it so happened that Thibaut, Count of Champagne and Brie, took the cross, and the Count Louis of Blois and Chartres likewise; and this was at the beginning of Advent (28th November 1199). Now you must know that this Count Thibaut was but a young man, and not more than twenty-two years of age, and the Count Louis not more than twenty-seven. These two counts were nephews and cousins-german to the King of France, and, on the other part, nephews to the King of England.

With these two counts there took the cross two very high and puissant barons of France, Simon of Montfort*, and Renaud of Montmirail. Great was the fame thereof throughout the land when these two high and puissant men took the cross.

[note: Simon de Monfort - the same one who later crushed the Albigensians and the father of the "English" Simon de Montfort who defeated the royal

army at Lewes and was killed at Evesham in 1265].

In the land of Count Thibaut of Champagne took the cross Garnier, Bishop of Troyes, Count Walter of Brienne, Geoffry of Joinville*, who was seneschal of the land, Robert his brother, Walter of Vignory, Walter of Montbéliard, Eustace of Conflans, Guy of Plessis his brother, Henry of Arzilliéres, Oger of Saint-Chéron, Villain of Neuilly, Geoffry of Villhardouin, Marshal of Champagne, Geoffry his nephew, William of Nully, Walter of Fuligny, Everard of Montigny, Manasses of l'Isle, Macaire of Sainte-Menehould, Miles the Brabant, Guy of Chappes, Clerembaud his nephew, Renaud of Dampierre, John Foisnous, and many other right worthy men whom this book does not here mention by name.

[note: Geoffry de Joinville - the father of the chronicler Joinville.]

With Count Louis took the cross Gervais of Châtel Hervée his son John of Virsin, Oliver of Rochefort, Henry of Mont-

3

reuil, Payen of Orléans, Peter of Bracietix, Hugh his brother, William of Sains, John of Frialze, Walter of Gaudonville, Hugh of Cormeray, Geoffry his brother, Hervée of Beauvoir, Robert of Frouville, Peter his brother, Orri of l'Isle, Robert of Quartier, and many more whom this book does not here mention by name.

In the Isle-de-France took the cross Nevelon, Bishop of Soissons, Matthew of Montmorency, Guy the Castellan of Coucy, his nephew, Robert of Ronsoi, Ferri of Yerres, John his brother, Walter of Saint-Denis, Henry his brother, William of Aunoi, Robert Mauvoisin, Dreux of Crcssonsacq, Bernard of Moreuil, Enguerrand of Boves, Robert his brother, and many more right worthy men with regard to whose names this book is here silent.

At the beginning of the following Lent, on the day when folk are marked with ashes (23rd February 1200), the cross was taken at Bruges by Count Baldwin of Flanders and Hainault, and by the Countess Mary his wife, who was sister to the Count Thibaut of Champagne. Afterwards took the cross, Henry his brother, Thierri his nephew, who was the son of Count Philip of Flanders, William the advocate of Béthune, Conon his brother, John of Nêle Castellan of Bruges, Renier of Trit, Reginald his son, Matthew of Wallincourt, James of Avesnes, Baldwin of Beauvoir, Hugh of Beaumetz, Gérard of Mancicourt, Odo of Ham, William of Gommegnies, Dreux of Beaurain, Roger of Marck, Eustace of Saubruic, Francis of Colemi, Walter of Bousies, Reginald of Mons, Walter of Tombes, Bernard of Somergen, and many more right worthy men in great number, with regard to whom this book does not speak further.

Afterwards took the cross, Count Hugh of St. Paul. With him took the cross, Peter of Amiens his nephew, Eustace of Canteleu, Nicholas of Mailly, Anscau of Cayeaux, Guy of Houdain, Walter of Nêle, Peter his brother, and many other men who are unknown to us.

Directly afterwards took the cross Geoffry of Perche, Stephen his brother, Rotrou of Montfort, Ives of La Jaille, Aimery of Villeroi, Geoffry of Beaumont, and many others whose names I do not know.

4

THE CRUSADERS SEND SIX ENVOYS TO VENICE

Afterwards the barons held a parliament at Soissons, to settle when they should start, and whither they should wend. But they could come to no agreement, because it did not seem to them that enough people had taken the cross. So during all that year (1200) no two months passed without assemblings in parliament at Compiègne. There met all the counts and barons who had taken the cross. Many were the opinions given and considered; but in the end it was agreed that envoys should be sent, the best that could be found, with full powers, as if they were the lords in person, to settle such matters as needed settlement.

Of these envoys, Thibaut, Count of Champagne and Brie, sent two; Baldwin, Count of Flanders and Hainault, two; and Louis, Count of Blois and Chartres, two. The envoys of the Count Thibaut were Geoffry of Villehardouin, Marshal of Champagne, and Miles the Brabant; the envoys of Count Baldwin were Conon of Béthune' and Alard Maquereau, and the envoys of Count Louis were John of Friaise, and Walter of Gaudonville.

To these six envoys the business in hand was fully committed, all the barons delivering to them valid charters, with seals attached, to the effect that they would undertake to maintain and carry out whatever conventions and agreements the envoys might enter into, in all sea ports, and whithersoever else the envoys might fare.

Thus were the six envoys despatched, as you have been told; and they took counsel among themselves, and this was their conclusion: that in Venice they might expect to find a greater number of vessels than in any other port. So they journeyed day by day, till they came thither in the first week of Lent (February 1201).

THE ENVOYS ARRIVE IN VENICE, AND PROFFER THEIR REQUEST

The Doge of Venice, whose name was Henry Dandolo* and

*[note: That Henry Dandolo was a very old man is certain, but there is doubt as to his precise age, as also as to the cause of his blindness. According to one account he had been blinded, or all but blinded, by the Greeks, and in a treacherous manner, when sent, at an earlier date, on an embassy to Constaritinople-whence his bitter hostility to the Greek Empire. I agree, however, with Sir Rennell Rodd that, if this had been so, Villehardouin would scarcely have refrained from mentioning such an act of perfidy on the part of the wicked Greeks. (See p. 41 of Vol 1of Sir Rennell Rodd's Princes of Achaia.) It is hardly to be imagined that he would keep the matter dark because, if he mentioned it, people would think Dandolo acted throughout from motives of personal vengeance. This would be to regard Villehardouin a- a very astute controversial historian indeed.]

5

who was very wise and very valiant, did them great honour, both he and the other folk, and entertained them right willingly, marvelling, however, when the envoys had delivered their letters, what might be the matter of import that had brought them to that country. For the letters were letters of credence only, and declared no more than that the bearers were to be accredited as if they were the counts in person, and that the said counts would make good whatever the six envoys should undertake.

So the Doge replied: " Signors, I have seen your letters; well do we know that of men uncrowned your lords are the greatest, and they advise us to put faith in what you tell us, and that they will maintain whatsoever you undertake. Now, therefore, speak, and let us know what is your pleasure."

And the envoys answered: " Sire, we would that you should assemble your council; and before your council we will declare the wishes of our lords; and let this be tomorrow, if it so pleases you." And the Doge replied asking for respite till the fourth day, when he would assemble his council, so that the envoys might state their requirements.

The envoys waited then till the fourth day, as had been appointed them, and entered the palace, which was passing rich and beautiful; and found the Doge and his council in a chamber. There they delivered their message after this manner: " Sire, we come to thee on the part of the high barons of France, who have taken the sign of the cross to avenge the shame done to Jesus Christ, and to reconquer Jerusalem, if so be that God -will suffer it. And because they know that no people have such great power to help them as you and your people, therefore we pray you by God that you take pity on the land overseas and the shame of Christ, and use diligence that our lords 'have ships for

5

transport and battle."

" And after what manner should we use diligence?

6

said the Doge. " After all manners that you may advise and propose," rejoined the envoys, " in so far as what you propose may be within our means." " Certes," said the Doge, " it is a great thing that your lords require of us, and well it seems that they have in view a high enterprise. We will give you our answer eight days from to-day. And marvel not if the term be long, for it is meet that so great a matter be fully pondered."

CONDITIONS PROPOSED BY THE DOGE

When the term appointed by the Doge was ended, the envoys returned to the palace. Many were the words then spoken which I cannot now rehearse. But this was the conclusion of that parliament: " Signors," said the Doge, " we will tell you the conclusions at which we have arrived, if so be that we can induce our great council and the commons of the land to allow of them; and you, on your part, must consult and see if you can accept them and carry them through.

" We will build transports* to carry four thousand five hundred horses, and nine thousand squires, and ships for four thousand five hundred knights, and twenty thousand sergeants of foot. And we will agree also to purvey food for these horses and people during nine months. This is what we undertake to do at the least, on condition that you pay us for each horse four marks, and for each man two marks.

[note: The old French term is vuissiers, *and denotes a kind of vessel, flat-bottomed, with large ports, specially constructed for the transport of horses. T. Smith translates "palanders," but I don't know that " palander" conveys any very clear idea to the English reader.]*

"And the covenants we are now explaining to you, we undertake to keep, wheresoever we may be, for a year, reckoning from the day on which we sail from the port of Venice in the service of God and of Christendom. Now the sum total of the expenses above named amounts to 85,000 marks.

"And this will we do moreover. For the love of God, we will add to the fleet fifty armed galleys on condition that, so long as we act in company, of all conquests in land or money, whether at sea or on dry ground, we shall have the half, and you the other half. Now consult together to see if you, on your parts, can accept and fulfil these covenants."

The envoys then departed, and said that they would consult together and give their answer on the morrow. They consulted, and talked together that night, and agreed to accept the terms offered. So the next day they appeared before the Doge, and said: " Sire, we are ready to ratify this covenant." The Doge thereon said he would speak of the matter to his people, and, as he found them affected, so would he let the envoys know the issue.

On the morning of the third day, the Doge, who was very wise and valiant, assembled his great council, and the council was of forty men of the wisest that were in the land. And the Doge, by his wisdom and wit, that were very clear and very good, brought them to agreement and approval. Thus he wrought with them; and then with a hundred others, then two hundred, then a thousand, so that at last all consented and approved. Then he assembled well ten thousand of the people in the church of St. Mark, the most beautiful church that there is, and bade them hear a mass of the Holy Ghost, and pray to God for counsel on the request and messages that had been addressed to them. And the people did so right willingly.

CONCLUSION OF THE TREATY, AND RETURN OF THE ENVOYS

When mass had been said, the Doge desired the envoys to humbly ask the people to assent to the proposed covenant. The envoys came into the church. Curiously were they looked upon by many who had not before had sight of them.

Geoffry of Villehardouin, the Marshal of Champagne, by will and consent of the other envoys, acted as spokesman and said unto them: " Lords, the barons of France, most high and puissant, have sent us to you; and they cry to you for mercy, that you take pity on Jerusalem, which is in bondage to the Turks, and that, for God's sake, you help to avenge the shame of Christ Jesus. And for this end they have elected to come to you, because they know full well that there is none other people having so great power on the seas, as you and your people. And they commanded us to fall at your feet, and not to rise till you consent to take pity on the Holy Land which is beyond the seas."

8

Then the six envoys knelt at the feet of the people, weeping many tears. And the Doge and all the others burst into tears of pity and compassion, and cried with one voice, and lifted up their hands, saying: " We consent, we consent I " Then was there so great a noise and tumult that it seemed as if the earth itself were falling to pieces.

And when this great tumult and passion of pity - greater did never any man see-were appeased, the good Doge of Venice, who was very wise and valiant, went up into the reading-desk, and spoke to the people, and said to them: "Signors, behold the honour that God has done you; for the best people in the world have set aside all other people, and chosen you to join them in so high an enterprise as the deliverance of our Lord!

All the good and beautiful words that the Doge then spoke, I cannot repeat to you. But the end of the matter was, that the covenants were to be made on the following day; and made they were, and devised accordingly. When they were concluded, it was notified to the council that we should go to Babylon (Cairo), because the Turks could better be destroyed in Babylon than in any other land; but to the folk at large it was only told that we were bound to go overseass. We were then in Lent (March 1201), and by St. john's Day, in the following year-which would be twelve hundred and two years after the Incarnation of Jesus Christ-the barons and pilgrims were to be in Venice, and the ships ready against their coming.

When the treaties were duly indited and sealed, they were brought to the Doge in the grand palace, where had been assembled the great and the little council. And when the Doge delivered the treaties to the envoys, he knelt greatly weeping, and swore on holy relics faithfully to observe the conditions thereof, and so did all his council, which numbered fifty-six persons. And the envoys, on their side, swore to observe the treaties, and in all good faith to maintain their oaths and the oaths of their lords; and be it known to you that for great pity many a tear was there shed. And forthwith were messengers sent to Rome, to the Pope Innocent, that he might confirm this covenant-the which he did right willingly.

Then did the envoys borrow five thousand marks of silver, and gave them to the Doge so that the building of the ships

9

might be begun. And taking leave to return to their own land, they journeyed day by day till they came to Placentia in Lombardy. There they parted. Geoffry, the Marshal of Champagne and Alard Maquereau went straight to France, and the others went to Genoa and Pisa to learn what help might there be had for the land overseass

When Geoffry, the Marshal of Champagne., passed over Mont Cenis, he came in with Walter of Brienne, going into Apulia, to conquer the land of his wife, whom he had married since he took the cross, and who was the daughter of King Tancred. With him went Walter of Montbéliard, and Eustace of

Conflans, Robert of Joinville, and a great part of the people of worth in Champagne who had taken the cross.

And when he told them the news how the envoys had fared, great was their joy, and much did they prize the arrangements made. And they said, " We are already on our way; and when you come, you will find us ready." But events fall out as God wills, and never had they power to join the host. This was much to our loss; for they were of great prowess and valiant. And thus they parted, and each went on his way.

So rode Geoffry the Marshal, day by day, that he came to Troyes in Champagne, and found his lord the Count Thibaut sick and languishing, and right glad was the count of his coming. And when he had told the count how he had fared, the count was so rejoiced that he said he would mount horse, a thing he had not done of a long time. So he rose from his bed and rode forth. But alas, how great the pity! For never again did he bestride horse but that once.

His sickness waxed and grew worse, so that at the last he made his will and testament, and divided the money which he would have taken with him on pilgrimage among his followers and companions, of whom he had many that were very good men and true-no one at that time had more. And he ordered that each one, on receiving his money, should swear on holy relics, to join the host at Venice, according as he had promised. Many there were who kept that oath badly, and so incurred great blame. The count ordered that another portion of his treasure should be retained, and taken to the host, and there expended as might seem best.

Thus died the count; and no man in this world made a better end. And there were present at that time a very

10

great assemblage of men of his lineage and of his vassals. But of the mourning and funeral pomp it is unmeet that I should here speak. Never was more honour paid to any man. And right well that it was so, for never was man of his age more beloved by his own men, nor by other folk. Buried he was beside his father in the church of our lord St. Stephen at Troyes. He left behind him the Countess, Ws wife, whose name was Blanche, very fair, very good, the daughter of the King of Navarre. She had borne him a little daughter, and was then about to bear a son.

THE CRUSADERS LOOK FOR ANOTHER CHIEF

When the Count was buried, Matthew of Montmorency, Simon ofMontfort,

Geoffry of Joinville who was seneschal, and Geoffry the Marshal, went to Odo, Duke of Burgundy, and said to him, " Sire, your cousin is dead. You see what evil has befallen the land overseass We pray you by God that you take the cross, and succour the land overseas in his stead. And we will cause you to have all his treasure, and will swear on holy relics, and make the others swear also, to serve you in all good faith, even as we should have served him."

Such was his pleasure that he refused. And be it known to you that he might have done much better. The envoys charged Geoffry of Joinville to make the self-same offer to the Count of Bar-le-Duc, Thibaut, who was cousin to the dead count, and he refused also.

Very great was the discomfort of the pilgrims, and of all who were about to go on God's service, at the death of Count Thibaut of Champagne; and they held a parliament, at the

beginning, of the month, at Soissons, to determine what they should do. There were present Count Baldwin of Flanders and Hainault, the Count Louis of Blois and Chartres, the Count Geoffry of Perche, the Count Hugh of Saint-Paul, and many other men of worth.

Geoffry the Marshal spake to them and told them of the offer made to the Duke of Burgundy, and to the Count of Bar-le-Duc, and how they had refused it. " My lords," said he, " listen, I will advise you of somewhat if you will

11

consent thereto. The Marquis of Montferrat* is very worthy and valiant, and one of the most highly prized of living men. If you asked him to come here, and take the sign of the cross and put himself in place of the Count of Champagne, and you gave him the lordship of the host, full soon would he accept thereof."

[note: Boniface, Marquis of Montferrat, was one of the most accomplished men of the time, and an approved soldier. His little court at Montferrat was the resort of artist and troubadour. His family was a family of Crusaders. The father, William of Montferrat, had gone overseass and fought valiantly against the infidel. Boniface's eldest brother, William of the Long Sword, married a daughter of the titular King of Jerusalem, and their son became titular king in turn. Another brother, Conrad, starting for the Holy Land, stopped at Constantinople, and did there such good service that the Greek emperor gave his sister to him in marriage; but afterwards fearing the perfidy of his brother-in-law, Conrad fled to Syria, and there battled against Saladin. Yet another brother, Renier, also served in the Greek Empire, married an Emperor's daughter, and received for guerdon of his deeds the kingdom of

Salonika. Boniface himself had fought valiantly against Saladin, been made prisoner, and afterwards liberated on exchange. It was no mean and nameless knight that Villehardouin was proposing as chief to the assembled Crusaders, but a princely noble, the patron of poets, verrsed in state affairs, and possessing personal experience of Eastern warfare. I extract these details from M. Bouchet's Notice].

Many were the words spoken for and against; but in the end all agreed, both small and great. So were letters written, and envoys chosen, and the marquis was sent for. And he came, on the day appointed, through Champagne and the Isle-de-France, where he received much honour, and specially from the King of France, who was his cousin.

BONIFACE, MARQUIS OF MONTFERRAT, BECOMES CHIEF OF THE CRUSADE - NEW CRUSADERS - DEATH OF GEOFFRY COUNT OF PERCHE

So he came to a parliament assembled at Soissons; and the main part of the counts and barons and of the other Crusaders were there assembled. When they heard that the marquis was coming, they went out to meet him, and did him much honour. In the morning the parliament was held in an orchard belonging to the abbey of our Lady of Soissons. There they besought the marquis to do as they had desired of him, and prayed him, for the love of God, to take the cross, and accept the leadership of the host, and stand in the place of Thibaut Count of Champagne, and accept of his money

12

and of his men. And they fell at his feet, with many tears; and he, on his part, fell at their feet, and said he would do it right willingly.

Thus did the marquis consent to their prayers, and receive the lordship of the host. Whereupon the Bishop of Soissons, and Master Fulk, the holy man, and two white monks whom the marquis had brought with him from Ws own land, led him into the Church of Notre Dame, and attached the cross to his shoulder. Thus ended this parliament, and the next day he took leave to return to his own land and settle his own affairs-telling them all to settle their own affairs likewise, for that he would meet them at Venice.

Thence did the marquis go to attend the Chapter at Citeaux, which is held on Holy Cross Day in September (14th September 1241). There he found a great number of abbots, barons and other people of Burgundy; and Master Fulk went thither to preach the Crusade. And at that place took the cross Odo the Champenois of Champlitte, and William his brother, Richard of Dampierre,

Odo his brother, Guy of Pesmes, Edmund his brother, Guy of Conflans, and many other good men of Burgundy, whose names are not recorded. Afterwards took the cross the Bishop of Autun, Guignes Count of Forez, Hugh of Bergi (father and son), Hugh of Colemi. Further on in Provence took the cross Peter Bromont, and many others whose names are unknown to us.

Thus did the pilgrims make ready in all lands. Alas! a great mischance befell them in the following Lent (March 1202) before they had started, for the Count Geoffry of Perche fell sick, and made his will in such fashion that he directed that Stephen, his brother, should have his goods, and lead his men in the host. Of this exchange the pilgrims would willingly have been quit, had God so ordered. Thus did the count make an end and die; and much evil ensued, for he was a baron high and honoured, and a good knight. Greatly was he mourned throughout all his lands.

FIRST STARTING OF THE PILGRIMS FOR VENICE, AND OF SOME WHO WENT NOT THITHER

After Easter and towards Whitsuntide (June 1202) began the pilgrims to leave their own country. And you must

know that at their departure many were the tears shed for

13

pity and sorrow, by their own people and by their friends. So they journeyed through Burgundy, and by the mountains of Mont-joux (? Jura) by Mont Cenis, and through Lombardy, and began to assemble at Venice, where they were lodged on an island which is called St. Nicholas in the port.

At that time started from Flanders a fleet that carried a great number of good men-at-arms. Of this fleet were captains John of Nêle, Castellan of Bruges, Thierri, who was the son of Count Philip of Flanders, and Nicholas of Mailly. And these promised Count Baldwin, and swore on holy relics, that they would go through the straits of Morocco, and join themselves to him, and to the host of Venice, at whatsoever place they might hear that the count was faring. And for this reason the Count of Flanders and Henry his brother had confided to them certain ships loaded with cloth and food and other wares.

Very fair was this fleet, and rich, and great was the reliance that the Count of Flanders and the pilgrims placed upon it, because very many of their good sergeants were journeying therein. But ill did these keep the faith they had sworn to the count, they and others like them, because they and such others of the same sort became fearful of the great perils that the host of Venice had undertaken.

Thus did the Bishop of Autun fail us, and Guignes the Count of Forez, and Peter Bromont, and many people besides, who were greatly blamed therein; and of little worth were the exploits they performed there where they did go. And of the French failed us Bernard of Moreuil, Hugh of Chaumont, Henry of Araines, John of Villers, Walter of Saint-Denis, Hugh his brother, and many others, who avoided the passage to Venice because of the danger, and went instead to Marseilles-whereof they received shame, and much were they blamed-and great were the mishaps that afterwards befell them.

OF THE PILGRIMS WHO CAME TO VENICE, AND OF THOSE WHO WENT TO APULIA

Now let us for this present speak of them no further, but speak of the pilgrims, of whom a great part had already come to Venice. Count Baldwin of Flanders had already arrived there, and many others, and thither were tidings brought to

14

them that many of the pilgrims were travelling by other ways, and from other ports. This troubled them greatly, because they would thus be unable to fulfil the promise made to the Venetians, and find the moneys that were due.

So they took counsel together, and agreed to send good envoys to meet the pilgrims, and to meet Count Louis of Blois and Chartres, who had not yet arrived, and to put them in good heart, and beseech them to have pity of the Holy Land beyond the sea, and show them that no other passage, save that from Venice, could be of profit.

For this embassy they made choice of Count Hugh of Saint-Paul and Geoffry the Marshal of Champagne, and these rode till they came to Pavia in Lombardy. There they found Count Louis with a great many knights and men of note and worth; and by encouragements and prayers prevailed on many to proceed to Venice who would otherwise have fared from other ports, and by other ways.

Nevertheless from Placentia many men of note proceeded by other ways to Apulia. Among them were Villain of Neuilly, who was one of the best knights in the world, Henry of Arzilliéres, Renaud of Dampierre, Henry of Longchamp, and Giles of Trasegnies, liegeman to Count Baldwin of Flanders and Hainault, who had given him, out of his own purse, five hundred *livres* to accompany him on this journey. With these went a great company of knights and sergeants, whose names are not recorded.

Thus was the host of those who went by Venice greatly weakened; and much evil befell them therefrom, as you shall shortly hear.

THE PILGRIMS LACK MONEY WHEREWITH TO PAY THE VENETIANS

Thus did Count Louis and the other barons wend their way to Venice; and they were there received with feasting and joyfully, and took lodging in the Island of St. Nicholas with those who had come before. Goodly was the host, and right worthy were the men. Never did man see goodlier or worthier. And the Venetians held a market, rich and abundant, of all things needful for horses and men. And the fleet they had got ready was so goodly and fine that never did Christian man see one goodlier or finer; as well galleys

15

as transports, and sufficient for at least three times as many men as were in the host.

Ah ! the grievous harm and loss when those who should have come thither sailed instead from other ports! Right well if they had kept their tryst, would Christendom have been exalted, and the land of the Turks abased! The Venetians had fulfilled all their undertakings, and above measure, and they now summoned the barons and counts to fulfil theirs and make payment, since they were ready to start.

The cost of each man's passage was now levied throughout the host; and there were people enough who said they could not pay for their passage, and the barons took from them such moneys as they had. So each man paid what he could. When the barons had thus claimed the cost of the passages, and when the payments had been collected, the moneys came to less than the sum due-yea, by more than one half.

Then the barons met together and said: "Lords, the Venetians have well fulfilled all their undertakings, and above measure. But we cannot fulfil ours in paying for our passages, seeing we are too few in number; and this is the fault of those who have journeyed by other ports. For God's sake therefore let each contribute all that he has, so that we may fulfil our covenant; for better is it that we should give all that we have, than lose what we have already paid, and prove false to our covenants; for if this host remains here, the rescue of the land overseas comes to naught."

Great was then the dissension among the main part of the barons and the other folk, and they said: " We have paid for our passages, and if they will take us, we shall go willingly; but if not, we shall inquire and look for other means of passage." And they spoke thus because they wished that the host should fall to pieces and each return to his own land. But the other party said, " Much rather would we give all that we have and go penniless with the host, than that the host should fall to pieces and fail; for God will doubtless repay us when it so pleases Him."

Then the Count of Flanders began to give all that he had and all that he could borrow, and so did Count Louis, and the Marquis, and the Count of Saint-Paul, and those who were of their party. Then might you have seen many a fine vessel of gold and silver borne in payment to the palace of the Doge. And when all had been brought together, there

16

was still wanting, of the sum required, 34,000 marks of silver. Then those who had kept back their possessions and not brought them into the common stock, were right glad, for they thought now surely the host must fail and go to pieces. But God, who advises those who have been ill-advised, would not so suffer it.

THE CRUSADERS OBTAIN A RESPITE BY PROMISING TO HELP THE VENETIANS AGAINST ZARA

Then the Doge spoke to his people, and said unto them:

Signors, these people cannot pay more; and in so far as they have paid at all, we have benefited by an agreement which they cannot now fulfil. But our right to keep this money would not everywhere be acknowledged; and if we so kept it we should be greatly blamed, both us and our land. Let us therefore offer them terms.

"The King of Hungary has taken from us Zara in Sclavonia, which is one of the strongest places in the world; and never shall we recover it with all the power that we possess, save with the help of these people. Let us therefore ask them to help us to reconquer it, and we will remit the payment of the debt of 34,000 marks of silver, until such time as it shall please God to allow us to gain the moneys by conquest, we and they together." Thus was agreement made. Much was it contested by those who wished that the host should be broken up. Nevertheless the agreement was accepted and ratified.

THE DOGE AND A NUMBER OF VENETIANS TAKE THE CROSS

Then, on a Sunday, was assemblage held in the church of St. Mark. It was a very high festival, and the people of the land were there, and the most part of the barons and pilgrims.

Before the beginning of High Mass, the Doge of Venice, who bore the name of Henry Dandolo, went up into the reading-desk, and spoke to the people, and said to them:" Signors, you are associated with the most worthy people in the world, and for the highest enterprise ever undertaken; and I am a man old and feeble, who should have need of rest, and I am sick in body; but I see that no one could command

17

and lead,you like myself, who am your lord. If you will consent that I take the sign of the cross to guard and direct you, and that my son remain in my place to guard the land, then shall I go to five or die with you and with the pilgrims."

And when they had heard him, they cried with one voice: "We pray you by God that you consent, and do it, and that you come with us! "

Very great was then the pity and compassion on the part of the people of the land and of the pil-rims; and many were the tears shed, because that worthy 0and good man would have had so much reason to remain behind, for he was an old man, and albeit his eyes were unclouded, yet he saw naught, having lost his sight through a wound in the head. He was of a great heart. Ah! how little like him were those who had gone to other ports to escape the danger.

Thus he came down from the reading-desk, and went before the altar, and knelt upon his knees greatly weeping. And they sewed the cross on to a great cotton hat, which he wore, in front, because he wished that all men should see it. And the Venetians began to take the cross in great numbers, a great multitude, for up to that day very few had taken the cross. Our pilgrims had much joy in the cross that the Doge took, and were greatly moved, because of the wisdom and the valour that were in him.

Thus did the Doge take the cross, as you have heard. Then the Venetians began to deliver the ships, the galleys, and the transports to the barons, for departure; but so much time had already been spent since the appointed term, that September drew near (1202).

MESSAGE OF ALEXIUS, THE SON OF ISAAC, THE DETHRONED EMPEROR OF CONSTANTINOPLE -DEATH OF FULK OF NEUILLY - ARRIVAL OF THE GERMANS

Now give ear to one of the greatest marvels, and most wonderful adventures that you have ever heard tell of. At that time there was an emperor in

Constantinople, whose name was Isaac, and he had a brothor, Alexius by name, whom he had ransomed from captivity among the Turks. This Alexius took his brother the emperor, tore the eyes out of his head, and made himself emperor by the aforesaid

18

treachery. He kept Isaac a long time in prison, together with a son whose name was Alexius. This son escaped from prison, and fled in a ship to a city on the sea, which is called Ancona. Thence he departed to go to King Philip of Germany, who had his sister for wife; and he came to Verona in Lombardy, and lodged in the town, and found there a number of pilgrims and other people who were on their way to join the host.

And those who had helped him to escape, and were with him, said: " Sire, here is an army in Venice, quite near to us, the best and most valiant people and knights that are in the world, and they are going overseass Cry to them therefore for mercy, that they have pity on thee and on thy father, who have been so wrongfully dispossessed. And if they be willing to help thee, thou shalt be guided by them. Perchance they will take pity on thy estate." And Alexius said he would do this right willingly, and that the advice was good.

Thus he appointed envoys, and sent them to the Marquis Boniface of Montferrat, who was chief of the host, and to the other barons. And when the barons saw them, they marvelled greatly, and said to the envoys: " We understand right well what you tell us. We will send an envoy with the prince to King Philip, whither he is going. If the prince will help to recover the land overseass we will help him to recover his own land, for we know that it has been wrested from him and from his father wrongfully." So were envoys sent into Germany, both to the heir of Constantinople and to King Philip of Germany.

Before this happened, of which I have just told you, there came news to the host which greatly saddened the barons and the other folk, viz., that Fulk, the good man, the holy man, who first preached the Crusade, had made an end and was dead.

And after this adventure, there came to the host a company of very good and worthy people from the empire of Germany, of whose arrival they of the host were full fain. There came the Bishop of Halberstadt, Count Berthold of Katzenelenbogen, Gamier of Borland, Thierri of Loos, Henry of Orme, Thierri of Diest, Roger of Suitre, Alexander of Villers, Ulric of Tone, and many other good folk, whose names are not recorded in this book.

19

THE CRUSADERS LEAVE VENICE TO BESIEGE ZARA

Then were the ships and transports apportioned by the barons. Ah, God I what fine war-horses were put therein. And when the ships were fulfilled with arms and provisions, and knights and sergeants, the shields were ranged round the bulwarks and castles of the ships, and the banners displayed, many and fair.

And be it known to you that the vessels carried more than three hundred petraries and mangonels, and all such engines as are needed for the taking of cities, in great plenty. Never did finer fleet sail from any0port. And this was in the octave of the Feast of St. Remigius (October) in the year of the Incarnation of Jesus Christ twelve hundred and two. Thus did they sail from the port of Venice, as you have been told.

On the Eve of St. Martin (10th November) they came before Zara in Sclavonia, and beheld the city enclosed by high walls and high towers; and vainly would you have sought for a fairer city, or one of greater strength, or richer. And when the pilgrims saw it, they marvelled greatly, and said one to another, " How could such a city be taken by force, save by the help of God himself? "

The first ships that came before the city cast anchor, and waited for the others; and in the morning the day was very fine and very clear, and all the galleys came up with the transports, and the other ships which were behind; and they took the port by force, and broke the chain that defended it and was very strong and well-wrought; and they landed in such sort that the port was between them and the town. Then might you have seen many a knight and many a sergeant swarming out of the ships, and taking from the transports many a good war-horse, and many a rich tent and many a pavilion. Thus did the host encamp. And Zara was besieged on St. Martin's Day (11th November 1202).

At this time all the barons had not yet arrived. Thus the Marquis of Montferrat had remained behind for some business that detained him. And Stephen of Perche had remained at Venice sick, and Matthew of Montmorency. When they were healed of their sickness Matthew of Montmorency came to rejoin the host at Zara; but Stephen of Perche dealt less worthily, for he abandoned the host, and

20

went to sojourn in Apulia. With him went Rotrou of Montfort and Ives of la jaille, and many others, who were much blamed therein; and they journeyed to Syria in the following spring.*

[note: Literally, "in the passaae of March," i.e. among the pilgrims who

THE INHABITANTS OF ZARA OFFER TO CAPITULATE, AND THEN DRAW BACK - ZARA IS TAKEN

On the day following the feast of St. Martin, certain of the people of Zara came forth, and spoke to the Doge of Venice, who was in his pavilion, and said to him that they would yield up the city and all their goods-their lives being spared-to his mercy. And the Doge replied that he would not accept these conditions, nor any conditions, save by consent of the counts and barons, with whom he would go and confer.

While he went to confer with the counts and barons, that party, of whom you have already heard, who wished to disperse the host, spoke to the envoys and said, " Why should you surrender your city? The pilgrims will not attack you -have no care of them. If you can defend yourselves against the Venetians, you will be safe enough." And they chose one of themselves, whose name was Robert of Boves, who went to the walls of the city, and spoke the same words. Therefore the envoys returned to the city, and the negotiations were broken off.

The Doge of Venice, when he came to the counts and barons, said to them: "Signors, the people who are therein desire to yield the city to my mercy, on condition only that their lives are spared. But I will enter into no agreement with them-neither this nor any other-save with your consent." And the barons answered: " Sire, we advise you to accept these conditions, and we even beg of you so to do." He said he would do so; and they all returned together to the pavilion of the Doge to make the agreement, and found that the envoys had gone away by the advice of those who wished to disperse the host.

Then rose the abbot of Vaux, of the order of the Cistercians, and said to them: " Lords, I forbid you, on the part of the Pope of Rome, to attack this city; for those within it

21

are Christians, and you are pilgrims." When the Doge heard this, he was very wroth, and much disturbed, and he said to the counts and barons: "Signors, I had this city, by their own agreement, at my mercy, and your people have broken that agreement; you have covenanted to help me to conquer it, and I summon you to do so."

Whereon the counts and barons all spoke at once, together with those who were of their party, and said: " Great is the outrage of those who have caused this agreement to be broken, and never a day has passed that they have not tried to break up the host. Now are we shamed if we do not help to take the city." And they came to the Doge, and said: " Sire, we will help you to take the city in despite of those who would let and hinder us."

Thus was the decision taken. The next morning the host encamped before the gates of the city, and set up their petraries and manoonels, and other engines of war, which they had in plenty, and on the side of the sea they raised ladders from the ships. Then they began to throw stones at the walls of the city and at the towers. So did the assault last for about five days. Then were the sappers set to mine one of the towers, and began to sap the wall. When those within the city saw this, they proposed an agreement, such as they had before refused by the advice of those who wished to break up the host.

THE CRUSADERS ESTABLISH THEMSELVES IN THE CITYAFFRAY BETWEEN THE VENETIANS AND THE FRANKS

Thus did the city surrender to the mercy of the Doge, on condition only that all lives should be spared. Then came the Doge to the counts and barons, and said to them: " Signors, we have taken this city by the grace of God, and your own. It is now winter, and we cannot stir hence till Eastertide; for we should find no market in any other place; and this city is very rich, and well furnished with all supplies. Let us therefore divide it in the midst, and we will take one half, and you the other."

As he had spoken, so was it done. The Venetians took the part of the city towards the port, where were the ships, and the Franks took the other part. There were quarters

22

assigned to each, according as was right and convenient. And the host raised the camp, and went to lodge in the city.

On the third day after they were all lodged, there befell a great misadventure in the host, at about the hour of vespers; for there began a fray, exceeding fell and fierce, between the Venetians and the Franks, and they ran to arms from all sides. And the fray was so fierce that there were but few streets in which battle did not rage with swords and lances and cross-bows and darts; and many people were killed and wounded.

But the Venetians could not abide the combat, and they began to suffer great losses. Then the men of mark, who did not want this evil to befall, came fully armed into the strife, and began to separate the combatants; and when they had separated them in one place, they began again in another. This lasted the better part of the night. Nevertheless with great labour and endurance at last they were separated. And be it known to you that this was the greatest misfortune that ever befell a host, and little did it lack that the host was not lost utterly. But God would not suffer it.

Great was the loss on either side. There was slain a high lord of Flanders, whose name was Giles of Landas: he was struck in the eye, and with that stroke he died in the fray; and many another of whom less was spoken. The Doge of Venice and the barons laboured much, during the whole of that week, to appease the fray, and they laboured so effectually that peace was made. God be thanked therefor.

ON WHAT CONDITIONS ALEXIUS PROPOSES TO OBTAIN THE HELP OF THE CRUSADERS FOR THE CONQUEST OF CONSTANTINOPLE

A fortnight after came to Zara the Marquis Boniface of Montferrat, who had not yet joined, and Matthew of Montmorency, and Peter of Bracieux, and many another man of note. And after another fortnight came also the envoys from Germany, sent by King Philip and the heir of Constantinople. Then the barons, and the Doge of Venice assembled in a palace where the Doge was lodged. And the envoys addressed them and said: " Lords, King Philip sends us to you, as does also the brother of the king's wife, the son of the emperor of Constantinople.

23

"'Lords,' says the king, ' I will send you the brother of my wife; and I commit him into the hands of God-may He keep him from death! - and into your hands. And because you have fared forth for God, and for right, and for justice, therefore you are bound, in so far as you are able, to restore to their own inheritance those who have been unrighteously despoiled. And my wife's brother will make with you the best terms ever offered to any people, and give you the most puissant help for the recovery of the land overseass

" ' And first, if God grant that you restore him to his inheritance, he will place the whole empire of Roumania in obedience to Rome, from which it has long been separated. Further, he knows that you have spent of your substance, and that you are poor, and he will give you 200,000 marks of silver, and food for all those of the host, both small and great. And he, of his own person, will go with you into the land of Babylon, or, if you hold that that will be better, send thither 10,000 men, at his own charges. And this service he will perform for one year. And all the days of his life he will maintain, at his own charges, five hundred knights in the land overseass to guard that land.' "

" Lords, we have full power," said the envoys, " to conclude this agreement, if you are willing to conclude it on your parts. And be it known to you, that so favourable an agreement has never before been offered to any one; and that he that would refuse it can have but small desire of glory and conquest."

The barons and the Doge said they would talk this over; and a parliament was called for the morrow. When all were assembled, the matter was laid before them.

DISCORD AMONG THE CRUSADERS - OF THOSE WHO ACCEPT THE PROPOSALS OF THE YOUNG ALEXIUS

Then arose much debate. The abbot of Vaux, of the order of the Cistercians, spoke, and that party that wished for the dispersal of the host; and they said they would never consent: that it was not to fall on Christians that they had left their homes, and that they would go to Syria.

And the other party replied: "Fair lords, in Syria you will be able to do nothing; and that you may right well perceive by considering how those have fared who abandoned us, and

24

sailed from other ports. And be it known to you that it is only by way of Babylon, or of Greece, that the land overseas can be recovered, if so be that it ever is recovered. And if we reject this covenant we shall be shamed to all time."

There was discord in the host, as you hear. Nor need you be surprised if there was discord among the laymen, for the white monks of the order of Citeaux were also at issue among themselves in the host. The abbot of Loos, who was a holy man and a man of note, and other abbots who held with him, prayed and besought the people, for pity's sake and the sake of God, to keep the host together, and agree to the proposed convention, in that " it afforded the best means by which the land overseas might be recovered; " while the abbot of Vaux, on the other hand, and those who held with him, preached full oft, and declared that all this was naught, and that the host ought to go to the land of Syria, and there do what they could.

Then came the Marquis of Montferrat, and Baldwin Count of Flanders and Hainault, and Count Louis, and Count Hugh of St. Paul, and those who held with them, and they declared that they would enter into the proposed covenant, for that they should be shamed if they refused. So they went to the Doge's hostel, and the envoys were summoned, and the covenant, in such terms as you have already heard, was confirmed by oath, and by charters with seals appended.

And the book tells you that only twelve persons took the oaths on the side of the Franks, for more (of sufficient note) could not be found. Among the twelve were first the Marquis of Montferrat, the Count Baldwin of Flanders, the Count Louis of Blois and of Chartres, and the Count of St. Paul, and eight others who held with them. Thus was the agreement made, and the charters prepared, and a term fixed for the arrival of the heir of Constantinople; and the term so Fixed was the fifteenth day after the following Easter.

OF THOSE WHO SEPARATED THEMSELVES FROM THE HOST TO GO TO SYRIA, AND OF THE FLEET OF THE COUNT OF FLANDERS

Thus did the host sojourn at Zara all that winter (1202-1203) in the face of the King of Hungary. And be it known to you that the hearts of the people were not at peace, for

25

the one party used all efforts to break up the host, and the other to make it hold together.

Many of the lesser folk escaped in the vessels of the merchants. In one ship escaped well nigh five hundred, and they were all drowned, and so lost. Another company escaped by land, and thought to pass through Sclavonia; and the peasants of that land fell upon them, and killed many, so that the remainder came back flying to the host. Thus did the host go greatly dwindling day by day. At that time a great lord of the host, who was from Germany, Garnier of Borland by name, so wrought that he escaped in a merchant vessel, and abandoned the host, whereby he incurred great blame.

Not long afterwards, a great baron of France, Renaud of Monmirail by name, besought so earnestly, with the countenance of Count Louis, that he was sent to Syria on an embassy in one of the vessels of the fleet; and he swore with his right hand on holy relics, he and all the knights who went with him, that within fifteen days after they had arrived in Syria, and delivered their message, they would return to the host. On this condition he left the host, and with him Hervée of Chitel, his nephew, William the *vidame* of Chartres, Geoffry of Beaumont, John of Frouville, Peter his brother, and many others. And the oaths that they swore were not kept; for they did not rejoin the host.

Then came to the host news that was heard right willingly, viz., that the fleet from Flanders, of which mention has been made above, had arrived at

Marseilles. And John of Nêle, Castellan of Bruges, who was captain of that host, and Thierri, who was the son of Count Philip of Flanders, and Nicholas of Mailly, advised the Count of Flanders, their lord, that they would winter at Marseilles, and asked him to let them know what was his will, and said that whatever was his will, that they would do. And he told them, by the advice of the Doge of Venice and the other barons, that they should sail at the end of the following March, and come to meet him at the port of Modon in Roumania. Alas! they acted very evilly, for never did they keep their word, but went to Syria, Where, as they well knew, they would achieve nothing.

Now be it known to you, lords, that if God had not loved the host, it could never have held together, seeing how many people wished evil to it!

26

THE CRUSADERS OBTAIN THE POPE'S ABSOLUTION FOR THE CAPTURE OF ZARA

Then the barons spoke together and said that they would send to Rome, to the Pope, because he had taken the capture of Zara in evil part. And they chose as envoys such as they knew were fitted for this office, two knights, and two clerks. Of the two clerks one was Nevelon, Bishop of Soissons, and the other Master John of Noyon, who was chancellor to Count Baldwin of Flanders; and of the knights one was John of Friaize, the other Robert of Boves. These swore on holy relics that they would perform their embassy loyally and in good faith, and that they would come back to the host.

Three kept their oath right well, and the fourth evilly, and this one was Robert of Boves. For he executed his office as badly as he could, and perjured himself, and went away to Syria as others had done. But the remaining three executed their office right well, and delivered their message as the barons had directed, and said to the Pope: " The barons cry mercy to you for the capture of Zara, for they acted as people who could do no better, owing to the default of those who had gone to other ports, and because, had they not acted as they did, they could not have held the host together. And as to this they refer themselves to you, as to their good Father, that you should tell them what are your commands, which they are ready to perform."

And the Pope said to the envoys that he knew full well that it was through the default of others that the host had been impelled to do this great mischief, and that he had them in great pity. And then he notified to the barons and pilgrims that he sent them his blessing, and absolved them as his sons, and commanded and besought them to hold the host together, inasmuch as he well knew that without that host God's service could not be done. And he gave full powers to

Nevelon, Bishop of Soissons, and Master John of Noyon, to bind and to unloose the pilgrims until the cardinal joined the host.

27

DEPARTURE OF THE CRUSADERS FOR CORFU - ARRIVAL OF THE YOUNG ALEXIUS - CAPTURE OF DURAS

So much time had passed that it was now Lent, and the host prepared their fleet to sail at Easter. When the ships were laden on the day after Easter (7th April 1203), the pilgrims encamped by the port, and the Venetians destroyed the city, and the walls and the towers.

Then there befell an adventure which weighed heavily upon the host; for one of the great barons of the host, by name Simon of Montfort, had made private covenant with the King of Hungary, who was at enmity with those of the host, and went to him, abandoning the host. With him went Guy of Montfort his brother, Simon of Nauphle and Robert Mauvoisin, and Dreux of Cressonsacq, and the abbot of Vaux, who was a monk of the order of the Cistercians, and many others. And not long after another great lord of the host, called Enguerrand of Boves, joined the King of Hungary, together with Hugh, Enguerrand's brother, and such of the other people of their country as they could lead away.

These left the host, as you have just heard; and this was a great misfortune to the host, and to such as left it a great disgrace.

Then the ships and transports began to depart; and it was settled that they should take port at Corfu, an island of Roumania, and that the first to arrive should wait for the last; and so it was done.

Before the Doge, the Marquis, and the galleys left Zara, Alexius, the son of the Emperor Isaac of Constantinople, had arrived together. He was sent by the King Philip of Germany, and received with great joy and great honour; and the Doge gave Mm as many galleys and ships as he required. So they left the port of Zara, and had a fair wind, and sailed onwards till they took port at Duras. And those of the land, when they saw their lord, yielded up the city right willingly and sware fealty to Mm.

And. they departed thence and came to Corfu, and found there the host encamped before the city; and those of the host had spread their tents and pavilions, and taken the horses out of the transports for ease and refreshment. When they heard that the son of the Emperor of Constantinople had arrived in the port, then might you have seen many a good knight and many a good sergeant leading many a good war-horse and going to meet him. Thus they received him with very great joy, and much high honour. And he had his tent pitched in the midst of the host; and quite near was pitched the tent of the Marquis of Montferrat, to whose ward he had been commended by King Philip, who had his sister to wife.

HOW THE CHIEFS OF THE CRUSADERS HELD BACK THOSE WHO WANTED TO ABANDON THE HOST

The host sojourned thus for three weeks in that island, which was very rich and plenteous. And while they sojourned, there happened a misadventure fell and grievous. For a great part of those who wished to break up the host, and had aforetime been hostile to it, spoke together and said that the adventure to be undertaken seemed very long and very perilous, and that they, for their part, would remain in the island, suffering the host to depart, and that-when the host had so departed-they would, through the people of Corfu, send to Count Walter of Brienne, who then held Brandis, so that he might send ships to take them thither.

I cannot tell you the names of all those who wrought in this matter, but I will name some among the most notable of the chiefs, viz., Odo of Champlitte, of Champagne, James of Avesnes, Peter of Amiens, Guy the Castellan of Coucy, Oger of Saint-Chéron, Guy of Chappes and Clerembaud his nephew, William of Aunoi, Peter Coiseau, Guy of Pesmes and Edmund his brother, Guy of Conflans, Richard of Dampierre, Odo his brother, and many more who had promised privily to be of their party, but who dared not for shame openly so to avow themselves; in such sort that the book testifies that more than half the host were in this mind.

And when the Marquis of Montferrat heard thereof, and Count Baldwin of Flanders, and Count Louis, and the Count of St. Paul, and the barons who held with them, they were greatly troubled, and said: " Lords, we are in evil case. If these people depart from us, after so many who have departed from us aforetime, our host is doomed, and we shall make no conquests. Let us then go to them, and fall at their feet, and cry to them for mercy, and for God's sake to have compas-

sion upon themselves and upon us, and not to dishonour themselves, and ravish from us the deliverance of the land overseass

Thus did the council decide; and they went, all together, to a valley where those of the other part were holding their parliament; and they took with them the son of the Emperor of Constantinople, and all the bishops and all the abbots of the host. And when they had come to the place they dismounted and went forward, and the barons fell at the feet of those of the other part, greatly weeping, and said they would not stir till those of the other part had promised not to depart from them.

And when those of the other part saw this, they were filled with very great compassion; and they wept very bitterly at seeing their lords, and their kinsmen, and their friends, thus lying at their feet. So they said they would consult together, and drew somewhat apart, and there communed. And the sum of their communing was this: that they would remain with the host till Michaelmas, on condition that the other part would swear, loyally, on holy relics, that from that day and thenceforward, at whatever hour they might be summoned to do so, they would in all good faith, and without guile, within fifteen days, furnish ships wherein the non-contents might betake themselves to Syria.

Thus was covenant made and sworn to; and then was there great joy throughout all the host. And all gat themselves to the ships, and the horses were put into the transports.

DEPARTURE FROM CORFU-CAPTURE OF ANDROS AND ABYDOS

Then did they sail from the port of Corfu on the eve of Pentecost (24th May), which was twelve hundred and three years after the Incarnation of our Lord Jesus Christ. And there were all the ships assembled, and all the transports, and all the galleys of the host, and many other ships of merchants that fared with them. And the day was fine and clear, and the wind soft and favourable, and they unfurled all their sails to the breeze.

And Geoffry, the Marshal of Champagne, who dictates this work, and has never lied therein by one word to his know-

30

ledge, and who was moreover present at all the councils held -he bears witness that never was yet seen so fair a sight. And well might it appear that such a fleet would conquer and gain lands, for, far as the eye could reach, there was no space without sails, and ships, and vessels, so that the hearts of men rejoiced greatly.

Thus they sailed over the sea till they came to Malea, to straits that are by the sea. And there they met two ships with pilgrims, and knights and sergeants returning from Syria, and they were of the parties that had gone to Syria by Marseilles. And when these saw our fleet so rich and well appointed, they conceived such shame that they dared not show themselves. And Count Baldwin of Flanders sent a boat from Ws ship to ask what people they were, and they said who they were.

And a sergeant let himself down from his ship into the boat, and said to those in the ship, " I cry quits to you for any goods of mine that may remain in the ship, for I am going with these people, for well I deem that they will conquer lands. "Much did we make of the sergeant, and gladly was he received in the host. For well may it be said, that even after following a thousand crooked ways a man may find his way right in the end.

The host fared forward till it came to Nigra (Negropont). Nigra is a very fair island, and there is on it a very good city called Negropont. Here the barons took council. Then went forward the Marquis Boniface of Montferrat, and Count Baldwin of Flanders and Hainault, with a great part of the transports and galleys, taking with them the son of the Emperor Isaac of Constantinople; and they came to an island called Andros, and there landed. The knights took their arms, and over-rode the country; and the people of the land came to crave mercy of the son of the Emperor of Constantinople, and gave so much of their goods that they made peace with Wm.

Then they returned to the ships, and sailed over the sea; when a great mishap befell, for a great lord of the host, whose name was Guy, Castellan of Coucy, died, and was cast into the sea.

The other ships, which had not sailed thitherward, had entered the passage of Abydos, and it is there that the straits of St. George (the Dardanelles) open into the great

31

sea. And they sailed up the straits to a city called Abydos, which lies on the straits of St. George, towards Turkey, and is very fair, and well situate. There they took port and landed, and those of the city came to meet them, and surrendered the city, as men without stomach to defend themselves. And such guard was established that those of the city lost not one stivercurrent.

They sojourned there eight days to wait for the ships transports and galleys that had not yet come up. And while they thus sojourned, they took corn from the land, for it was the season of harvest, and great was their need thereof, for before they had but little. And within those eight days all the ships and barons had come up. God gave them fair weather.

ARRIVAL AT ST. STEPHEN - DELIBERATION AS TO PLAN OF ATTACK

All started from the port of Abydos together. Then might you have seen the Straits of St. George (as it were) in flower with ships and galleys sailing upwards, and the beauty thereof was a great marvel to behold. Thus they sailed up the Straits of St. George till they came, on St. John the Baptist's Eve, in June (23rd June 1203) to St. Stephen, an abbey that lay three leagues from Constantinople. There had those on board the ships and galleys and transports full sight of Constantinople; and they took port and anchored their vessels.

Now you may know that those who had never before seen Constantinople looked upon it very earnestly, for they never thought there could be in all the world so rich a city; and they marked the high walls and strong towers that enclosed it round about, and the rich palaces, and mighty churches of which there were so many that no one would have believed it who had not seen it with his eyes-and the height and the length of that city which above all others was sovereign. And be it known to you, that no man there was of such hardihood but his flesh trembled: and it was no wonder, for never was so great an enterprise undertaken by any people since the creation of the world.

Then landed the counts and barons and the Doge of Venice, and a parliament was held in the church of St. -

32

Stephen. There were many opinions set forth, this way and that. All the words then spoken shall not be recorded in this book; but in the end the Doge rose on his feet and said: "Signors, I know the state of this land better than you do, for I have been here erewhile. We have undertaken the greatest enterprise, and the most perilous, that ever people have undertaken. Therefore it behoves us to go to work warily. Be it known to you that if we go on dry ground, the land is great and large, and our people are poor and ill-provided. Thus they will disperse to look for food; and the people of the land are in great multitude, and we cannot keep such good watch but that some of ours will be lost. Nor are we in case to lose any, for our people are but few indeed for the work in hand.

"Now there are islands close by which you can see from here, and these are inhabited, and produce corn, and food, and other things. Let us take port there, and gather the corn and provisions of the land. And when we have collected our supplies, let us go before the city, and do as our Lord shall provide. For he that has supplies, wages war with more certainty than he that has none. "To this counsel the lords and barons agreed, and all went back to their ships and vessels.

THE CRUSADERS LAND AT CHALCEDON AND SCUTARI

They rested thus that night. And in the morning, on the day of the feast of our Lord St. John the Baptist in June (24th June 1203), the banners and pennants were flown on the castles of the ships, and the coverings taken from the shields, and the bulwarks of the ships garnished. Every one looked to his antis, such as he should use, for well each man knew that full soon he would have need of them.

The sailors weighed the anchors, and spread the sails to the wind, and God gave them a good wind, such as was convenient to them. Thus they passed before Constantinople, and so near to the walls and towers that we shot at many of their vessels. There were so many people on the walls and towers that it seemed as if there could be no more people (in the world).

Then did God our Lord set to naught the counsel of the day before, and keep us from sailing to the islands: that counsel

33

fell to naught as if none had ever heard thereof. For lo, our ships made for the mainland as straight as ever they could, and took port before a palace of the Emperor Alexius, at a place called Chalcedon. This was in face of Constantinople, on the other side of the straits,. towards Turkey. The palace was one of the most beautiful and delectable that ever eyes could see, with every delight therein that the heart of man could desire, and convenient for the house of a prince.

The counts and barons landed and lodged themselves in the palace; and in the city round about, the main part pitched their tents. Then were the horses taken out of the transports, and the knights and sergeants got to land with all their arms, so that none remained in the ships save the mariners only. The country was fair, and rich) and well supplied with all good things, and the sheaves of corn (which had been reaped) were in the fields, so that all-and they stood in no small need-might take thereof.

Thev soioumed thus in that palace the following day; and on the third day God gave them a good wind, and the mariners raised their anchors, and spread their sails to the wind. They went thus up the straits, a good league above Constantinople, to a palace that belonged to the Emperor Alexius, and was called Scutari. There the ships anchored, and the transports, and all the galleys. The horsemen who had lodged in the palace of Chalcedon went along the shore by land.

The host of the French encamped thus on the straits of St. George, at Scutari, and above it. And when the Emperor Alexius saw this, he caused his host to issue from Constantinople, and encamp over against us on the other side of the straits, and there pitched his tents, so that we might not take land against him by force. The host of the French sojourned thus for nine days, and those obtained supplies who needed them, and that was every one in the host.

THE FORAGERS DEFEAT THE GREEKS

During this time, a company of good and trustworthy men issued (from the camp) to guard the host, for fear it should be attacked, and the foragers searched the country. In the said company were Odo of Champlitte, of Champagne, and William his brother, and Oger of Saint-Chéron, and

34

Manasses of l'Isle, and Count Girard, a count of Lombardy, a retainer of the Marquis of Montferrat; and they had with them at least eighty knights who were good men and true.

And they espied, at the foot of a mountain, some three leagues distant from the host, certain tents belonging to the Grand Duke of the Emperor of Constantinople, who had with him at least five hundred Greek knights. When our people saw them, they formed their men into four battalions, and decided to attack. And when the Greeks saw this, they formed their battalions, and arrayed themselves in rank before their tents, and waited. And our people went forward and fell upon them right vigorously.

By the help of God our Lord, this fight lasted but a little while, and the Greeks turned their backs. They were discomfited at the first onset, and our people pursued them for a full great league. There they won plenty of horses and stallions, and palfreys, and mules, and tents and pavilions, and such spoil as is usual in such case. So they returned to the host, where they were right well received, and their spoils were divided, as was fit.

MESSAGE OF THE EMPEROR ALEXIUS-REPLY OF THE CRUSADERS

The next day after, the Emperor Alexius sent an envoy with letters to the counts and to the barons. This envoy was called Nicholas Roux, and he was a native of Lombardy. He found the barons in the rich palace of Scutari, where they were holding council and he saluted them on the part of the Emperor

Alexius of Constantinople, and tendered his letters to the Marquis of Montferrat-who received them. And the letters were read before all the barons; and there were in them words, written after various manners, which the book does not (here) relate, and at the end of the other words so written, came words of credit, accrediting the bearer of the letters, whose name was Nicholas Roux.

"Fair Sir," said the barons, "we have seen your letters, and they tell us that we are to give credit to what you say, and we credit you right well. Now speak as it pleases you."

And the envoy was standing before the barons, and spoke thus: "Lords," said he, "the Emperor Alexius would have you know that he is well aware that you are the best people

35

uncrowned, and come from the best land on earth. And he marvels much why, and for what purpose, you have come into his land and kingdom. For you are Christians, and he is a Christian, and well he knows that you are on your way to deliver the Holy Land overseass and the Holy Cross, and the Sepulchre. If you are poor and in want, he will right willmgly give you of his food and substance, provided you depart out of his land. Neither would he otherwise wish to do you any hurt, though he has full power therein, seeing that if you were twenty times as numerous as you are, you would not be able to get away without utter discomfiture if so be that he wished to harm you."

By agreement and desire of the other barons, and of the Doge of Venice, then rose to his feet Conon of Béthune, who was a good knight, and wise, and very eloquent, and he replied to the envoy: " Fair Sir, you have told us that your lord marvels much why our signors and barons should have entered into Ms kingdom and land. Into his land they have not entered, for he holds this land wrongfully and wickedly, and against God and against reason. It belongs to Ws nephew, who sits upon a throne among us, and is the son of his brother, the Emperor Isaac. But if he is willing to throw himself on the mercy of his nephew, and to give Mm back his crown and empire, then we will pray his nephew to forgive him, and bestow upon him as much as will enable him to live wealthily. And if you come not as the bearer of such a message, then be not so bold as to come here again." So the envoy departed and went back to Constantinople, to the Emperor Alexius.

THE CRUSADERS SHOW THE YOUNG ALEXIUS TO THE PEOPLE OF CONSTANTINOPLE, AND PREPARE FOR THE BATTLE

The barons consulted together on the morrow, and said that they would show the young Alexius, the son of the Emperor of Constantinople, to the people of the city. So they assembled all the galleys. The Doge of Venice and the Marquis of Montferrat entered into one, and took with them Alexius, the son of the Emperor Isaac; and into the other galleys entered the knights and barons, as many as would.

They went thus quite close to the walls of Constantinople and showed the youth to the people of the Greeks, and said,

36

"Behold your natural lord; and be it known to you that we have not come to do you harm, but have come to guard and defend you, if so be that you return to your duty. For he whom you now obey as your lord holds rule by wrong and wickedness, against God and reason. And you know full well that he has dealt treasonably with him who is your lord and his brother, that he has blinded his eyes and reft from him his empire by wrong and wickedness. Now behold the rightful heir. If you hold with him, you will be doing as you ought; and if not we will do to you the very worst that we can." But for fear and terror of the Emperor Alexius, not one person on the land or in the city made show as if he held for the prince. So all went back to the host, and each sought his quarters.

On the morrow, when they had heard mass, they assembled in parliament, and the parliament was held on horseback in the midst of the fields. There might you have seen many a fine war-horse, and many a good knight thereon. And the council was held to discuss the order of the battalions, how many they should have, and of what strength. Many were the words said on one side and the other. But in the end it was settled that the advanced guard should be given to Baldwin of Flanders, because he had a very great number of good men, and archers and crossbowmen, more than any other chief that was in the host.

And after, it was settled that Henry his brother, and Matthew of Wallincourt, and Baldwin of Beauvoir, and many other good knights of their land and country, should form the second division.

The third division was formed by Count Hugh of St. Paul, Peter of Amiens his nephew, Eustace of Canteleu, Anseau of Cayeux, and many good knights of their land and country.

The fourth division was formed by Count Louis of Blois and Chartres, and was very numerous and rich and redoubtable; for he had placed therein a great number of good knights and men of worth.

The fifth division was formed by Matthew of Montmorency and the men of Champagne. Geoffry the Marshal of Champagne formed part of it, and Oger of Saint-Chéron, Manasses of l'Isle, Miles the Brabant, Macaire of Sainte-Menehould, John Foisnous, Guy of Chappes, Clerembaud his nephew, Robert of Ronsoi; all these people formed part of the fifth

37

division. Be it known to you that there was many a good knighttherein.

The sixth division was formed by the people of Burgundy. In this division were Odo the Champenois of Champlitte, William his brother, Guy of Pesmes, Edmund his brother, Otho of la Roche, Richard of Dampierre, Odo his brother, Guy of Conflans, and the people of their land and country.

The seventh division, which was very large, was under the command of the Marquis of Montferrat. In it were the Lombards and Tuscans and the Germans, and all the people who were from beyond Mont Cenis to Lyons on the Rhone. All these formed part of the division under the marquis, and it was settled that they should form the rearguard.

THE CRUSADERS SEIZE THE PORT

The day was fixed on which the host should embark on the ships and transports to take the land by force, and either live or die. And be it known to you that the enterprise to be achieved was one of the most redoubtable ever attempted. Then did the bishops and clergy speak to the people, and tell them how they must confess, and make each one his testament, seeing that no one knew what might be the will of God concerning him. And this was done right willingly throughout the host, and very piously.

The term fixed was now come; and the knights went on board the transports with their war-horses; and they were fully armed, with their helmets laced, and the horses covered with their housings, and saddled. All the other folk, who were of less consequence in battle, were on the great ships; and the galleys were fully armed and made ready.

The morning was fair a little after the rising of the sun; and the Emperor Alexius stood waiting for them on the other side, with great forces, and everything in order. And the trumpets sound, and every galley takes a transport in tow, so as to reach the other side more readily. None ask who shall go first, but each makes the land as soon as he can. The knights issue from the transports, and leap into the sea up to their waists, fully armed, with helmets laced, and lances in hand; and the good archers, and the good sergeants, and the good crossbowmen, each in his company, land so soon as they touch ground.

38

The Greeks made a goodly show of resistance; but when it came to the lowering of the lances, they turned their backs, and went away flying, and abandoned the shore. And be it known to you that never was port more proudly taken. Then began the mariners to open the ports of the transports, and let down the bridges, and take out the horses; and the knights began to mount, and they began to marshal the divisions of the host in due order.

CAPTURE OF THE TOWER OF GALATA

Count Baldwin of Flanders and Hainault, with the advanced guard, rode forward, and the other divisions of the host after him, each in due order of march; and they came to where the Emperor Alexius had been encamped. But he had turned back towards Constantinople, and left his tents and pavilions standing. And there our people had much spoil.

Our barons were minded to encamp by the port before the tower of Galata, where the chain was fixed that closed the port of Constantinople. And be it known to you, that any one must perforce pass that chain before he could enter into the port. Well did our barons then perceive that if they did not take the tower, and break the chain, they were but as dead men, and in very evil case. So they lodged that night before the tower, and in the Jewry that is called Stenon, where there was a good city, and very rich.

Well did they keep guard during the night; and on the morrow, at the hour of tierce, those who were in the tower of Galata made a sortie, and those who were in Constantinople came to their help in barges; and our people ran to arms. There came first to the onset James of Avesnes and his men on foot; and be it known to you that he was fiercely charged, and wounded by a lance in the face, and in peril of death. And one of his knights, whose name was Nicholas of Jenlain, gat to horse, and came to his lord's rescue, and succoured him right well, and so won great honour.

Then a cry was raised in the host, and our people ran together from all sides, and drove back the foe with great fury, so that many were slain and taken. And some of them did not go back to the tower, but ran to the barges by which they had come, and there many were drowned, and some escaped.

39

As to those who went back to the tower, the men of our host pressed them so hard that they could not shut the gate. Then a terrible fight began again at the gate, and our people took it by force, and made prisoners of all those in the tower. Many were there killed and taken.

ATTACK ON THE CITY BY LAND AND SEA

So was the tower of Galata taken, and the port of Constantinople won by force. Much were those of the host comforted thereby, and much did they praise the Lord God; and greatly were those of the city discomforted. And on the next day, the ships, the vessels, the galleys and the transports were drawn into the port.

Then did those of the host take council together to settle what thing they should do, and whether they should attack the city by sea or by land. The Venetians were firmly minded that the scaling ladders ought to be planted on the ships, and all the attack made from the side by the sea. The French, on the other hand, said that they did not know so well how to help themselves on sea as on land, but that when they had their horses and their arms they could help themselves on land right well. So in the end it was devised that the Venetians should attack by sea, and the barons and those of the host by land.

They sojourned thus for four days. On the fifth day, the whole host were armed, and the divisions advanced on horseback, each in the order appointed, along the harbour, till they came to the palace of Blachernae; and the ships drew inside the harbour till they came over against the self-same place, and this was near to the end of the harbour. And there is at that place a river that flows into the sea, and can only be passed by a bridge of stone. The Greeks had broken down the bridge, and the barons caused the host to labour all that day and all that night in repairing the bridge. Thus was the bridge repaired, and in the morning the divisions were armed, and rode one after the other in the order appointed, and came before the city. And no one came out from the city against them; and this was a great marvel, seeing that for every man that was in the host there were over two hundred men in the city.

Then did the barons decide that they should quarter them-

40

selves between the palace of Blachernae and the castle of Boemond, which was an abbey enclosed with walls. So the tents and pavilions were pitched-which was a right proud thing to look upon; for of Constantinople, which had three leagues of front towards the land, the whole host could attack no more than one of the gates. And the Venetians lay on the sea, in ships and vessels, and raised their ladders, and mangonels, and petraries, and made order for their assault right well. And the barons for their part made ready their petraries and mangonels on land.

And be it known to you that they did not have their time in peace and quiet; for there passed no hour of the night or day but one of the divisions had to stand armed before the gate, to guard the engines, and provide against attack. And, notwithstanding all this, the Greeks ceased not to attack them, by this gate and by others, and held them so short that six or seven times a day the whole host was forced to run to arms. Nor could they forage for provisions more than four bow-shots' distance from the camp. And their stores were but scanty, save of flour and bacon, and of those they had a little; and of fresh meat none at all, save what they got from the horses that were killed. And be it known to you that there was only food generally in the host for three weeks. Thus were they in very perilous case, for never did so few people besiege so many people in any city.

FIRST INCIDENTS OF THE ASSAULT

Then did they bethink themselves of a very good device; for they enclosed the whole camp with good lists, and good palisades, and good barriers, and were thus far stronger and much more secure. The Greeks meanwhile came on to the attack so frequently that they gave them no rest, and those of the host drove them back with great force; and every time that the Greeks issued forth they lost heavily.

One day the Burgundians were on guard, and the Greeks made an attack upon them, with part of the best forces that they had. And the Burgundians ran upon the Greeks and drove them in very fiercely, and followed so close to the gate that stones of great weight were hurled upon them. There was taken one of the best Greeks of the city, whose name was Constantine Lascaris; William of Neuilly took him all

41

mounted upon his horse. And there did William of Champlitte have his arm broken with a stone, and great pity it was, for he was very brave and very valiant.

I 'cannot tell you of all the good strokes that were there stricken, nor of all the wounded, nor all the dead. But before the fight was over, there came into it a knight of the following of Henry, the brother, of Count Baldwin of Flanders and Hainault, and his name was Eustace of Marchais; and he was armed only in padded vest and steel cap, with his shield at his neck; and he did so well in the fray that he won to himself great honour. Few were the days on which no sorties were made; but I cannot tell you of them all. So hardly did they hold us, that we could not sleep, nor rest, nor eat, save in arms.

Yet another sortie was made from a gate further up; and there again did the Greeks lose heavily. And there a knight was slain, whose name was William of Gi; and there Matthew of Wallincourt did right well, and lost his horse, which was killed at the drawbridge of the gate; and many others who were in that fight did right well. From this gate, which was beyond the palace of Blachernae, the Greeks issued most frequently, and there Peter of Bracieux gat himself more honour than any, because he was quartered the nearest, and so came most often into the fray.

ASSAULT OF THE CITY

Thus their peril and toil lasted for nearly ten days, until, on a Thursday morning (17th July 1203) all things were ready for the assault, and the ladders in trim; the Venetians also had made them ready by sea. The order of the assault was so devised, that of the seven divisions, three were to guard the camp outside the city, and other four to give the assault. The Marquis Boniface of Montferrat guarded the camp towards the fields, with the division of the Burgundians, the division of the men of Champagne, and Matthew of Montmorency. Count Baldwin of Flanders and Hainault went to the assault with his people, and Henry his brother; and . Count Louis of Blois and Chartres, and Count Hugh of St. Paul, and those who held with them, went also to the assault.

They planted two ladders at a barbican near the sea; and the wall was well defended by Englishmen and Danes; and

42

the attack was stiff and good and fierce. By main strength certain knights and two sergeants got up the ladders and made themselves masters of the wall; and at least fifteen got upon the wall, and fought there, hand to hand, with axes and swords, and those within redoubled their efforts and cast them out in very ugly sort, keeping two as prisoners' And those of our people who had been taken were led before the Emperor Alexius; much was he pleased thereat. Thus did the assault leave matters on the side of the French. Many were wounded and many had their bones broken, so that the barons were very wroth.

Meanwhile the Doge of Venice had not forgotten to do his part, but had ranged his ships and transports and vessels in line, and that line was well three crossbow-shots in length; and the Venetians began to draw near to the part of the shore that lay under the walls and the towers. Then might you have seen the mangonels shooting from the -ships and transports, and the crossbow bolts flying, and the bows letting fly their arrows deftly and well; and those within defending the walls and towers very fiercely; and the ladders on the ships coming so near that in many places swords and lances crossed; and the tumult and noise were so great that it seemed as if the very earth and sea were melting together. And be it known to you that the galleys did not dare to come to the shore.

CAPTURE OF TWENTY-FIVE TOWERS

Now may you hear of a strange deed of prowess; for the Doge of Venice, who was an old man, and saw naught (seeing he was blind), stood, fully armed, on the prow of his galley, and had the standard of St. Mark before him; and he cried to his people to put him on land, or else that he would do justice upon their bodies with his hands. And so they did, for the galley was run aground, and they leapt therefrom, and bore the standard of St. Mark before him on to the land.

And when the Venetians saw the standard of St. Mark on land, and the galley of their lord touching ground before them, each held himself for shamed, and they all gat to the land; and those in the transports leapt forth, and landed; and those in the big ships got into barges, and made for the shore, each and all as best they could. Then might you have

43

seen an assault, great and marvellous; and to this bears witness Geoffry of Villehardouin, who makes this book, that more than forty people told him for sooth that they saw the standard of St. Mark of Venice at the top of one of the towers, and that no man knew who bore it thither.

Now hear of a strange miracle: those who are within the city fly and abandon the walls, and the Venetians enter in, each as fast and as best he can, and seize twenty-five of the towers, and man them with their people. And the Doge takes a boat, and sends messengers to the barons of the host to tell them that lie has taken twenty-five towers, and that they may know for sooth that such towers cannot be retaken. The barons are so overjoyed that they cannot believe their ears; and the Venetians begin to send to the host in boats the horses and palfreys they have taken.

When the Emperor Alexius saw that our people had thus entered into the city, he sent his people against them in such numbers that our people saw they would be unable to endure the onset. So they set fire to the buildings between them and the Greeks; and the wind blew from our side, and the fire began to wax so great that the Greeks could not see our people who retired to the towers they had seized and conquered.

THE EMPEROR ALEXIUS COMES OUT FOR BATTLE, BUT RETIRES WITHOUT ATTACKING

Then the Emperor Alexius issued from the city, with all his forces, by other gates which were at least a league from the camp; and so many began to issue forth that it seemed as if the whole world were there assembled. The emperor marshalled his troops in the plain, and they rode towards the camp; and when our Frenchmen saw them coming, they ran to arms from all sides. On that day Henry, the brother of Count Baldwin of Flanders, was mounting guard over the engines of war before the gate of Blachernae, together with Matthew of Wallincourt, and Baldwin of Beauvoir, and their followers. Against their encampment the Emperor Alexius had made ready a great number of his people, who were to issue by three gates, while he himself should fall upon the host from another side.

Then the six divisions issued from our camp as had been

44

devised, and were marshalled in ranks before the palisades: the sergeants and squires on foot behind the horses, and the archers and crossbowmen in front. And there was a division of the knights on foot, for we had at least two hundred who, were without horses. Thus they stood still before the palisades. And this showed great good sense, for if they had moved to the attack, the numbers of the enemy were such that they must have been overwhelmed and (as it were) drowned among them.

It seemed as if the whole plain was covered with troops, and they advanced slowly and in order. Well might we appear in perilous case, for we had but six divisions, while the Greeks had full forty, and there was not one of their divisions but was larger than any of ours. But ours were ordered in such sort that none could attack them save in front. And the Emperor Alexius rode so far for-ward that either side could shoot at the other. And when the Doge of Venice heard this, he made his people come forth, and leave the towers they had taken, and said he would live or die with the pilgrims. So he came to the camp, and was himself the first to land, and brought with him such of his people as he could.

Thus, for a long space, the armies of the pilgrims and of the Greeks stood one against the other; for the Greeks did not dare to throw themselves upon our ranks, and our people would not move from their palisades. And when the Emperor Alexius saw this, he began to withdraw his people, and when he had rallied them, he turned back. And seeing this, the host of the pilgrims began to march towards him with slow steps, and the Greek troops began to move backwards, and retreated to a palace called Philopas.

And be it known to you, that never did God save any people from such peril as He saved the host that day; and be it known to you further that there was none in the host so hardy but he had great joy thereof. Thus did the battle remain for that day. As it pleased God nothing further was done. The Emperor Alexius returned to the city, and those of the host to their quarters-the latter taking off their armour, for they were weary and overwrought; and they ate and drank little, seeing that their store of food was but scanty.

45

ALEXIUS ABANDONS CONSTANTINOPLE - HIS BROTHER ISAAC IS REPLACED ON THE THRONE - THE CRUSADERS SEND HIM A MESSAGE

Now listen to the miracles of our Lord-how gracious are they whithersoever it pleases Him to perform them! That very might the Emperor Alexius of Constantinople took of his treasure as much as he could carry, and took with him as many of his people as would go, and so fled and abandoned the city. And those of the city remained astonied, and they drew to the prison in which lay the Emperor Isaac, whose eyes had been put out. Him they clothed imperially, and bore to the great palace of Blachernae, and seated on a high throne; and there they did to him obeisance as their lord. Then they took messengers, by the advice of the Emperor Isaac, and sent them to the host, to apprise the son of the Emperor Isaac, and the barons, that the Emperor Alexius had fled, and that they had again raised up the Emperor Isaac as emperor.

When the young man knew of this he summoned the Marquis Boniface of Montferrat, and the marquis summoned the barons throughout the host. And when they were met in the pavilion of the Emperor Isaac's son, he told them the news. And when they heard it, their joy was such as cannot be uttered, for never was greater joy in all this world. And greatly and most devoutly was our Lord praised by all, in that He had succoured them within so short a term, and exalted them so high from such a low estate. And therefore well may one say: " Him whom God will help can no man injure."

Then the day began to dawn, and the host to put on their armour; and all gat them to their arms throughout the host, because they did not greatly trust the Greeks. And messengers began to come out from the city, two or three together, and told the same tale. The barons and counts, and the Doge of Venice had agreed to send envoys into the city, to know how matters really stood; and, if that was true which had been reported, to demand of the father that he should ratify the covenants made by the son; and, if he would not, to, declare that they on their part should not suffer the son to enter into the city. So envoys were chosen: one was

Matthew of Montmorency, and Geoffry the Marshal of Champagne was the other, and two Venetians on the part of the Doge of Venice.

The envoys were conducted to the gate, and the gate was opened to them, and they dismounted from their horses. The Greeks had set Englishmen and Danes, with their axes, at the gate and right up to the palace of Blachernae. Thus were the envoys conducted to the great palace. There they found the Emperor Isaac, so richly clad that you would seek in vain throughout the world for a man more richly apparelled than he, and by his side the empress, his wife, a most fair lady, the sister of the King of Hungary; and of great men and great ladies there were so many, that you could not St' ir foot for the press, and the ladies were so richly adorned that richer adornment might not be. And all those who, the day before, had been against the emperor were, on that day, subject in everything to his good pleasure.

THE EMPEROR ISAAC RATIFIES THE COVENANTS ENTERED INTO BY HIS SON

The envoys came before the Emperor Isaac, and the emperor and all those about him did them great honour. And the envoys said that they desired to speak to him privily, ,on the part of his son, and of the barons of the host. And he rose and entered into a chamber, and took with him only the empress, and his chancellor, and his dragoman (interpreter) and the four envoys. By consent of the other envoys, Geoffry of Villehardouin, the Marshal of Champagne, acted as spokesman, and he said to the Emperor Isaac: " Sire, thou seest the service we have rendered to thy son, and how we have kept our covenants with him. But he cannot come hither till he has given us surety for the covenants he has made with us. And he asks of thee, as thy son, to confirm those covenants in the same form, and the same manner, that he has done." " What covenants are they? " said the emperor. " They are such as we shall tell you," replied the envoys: " In the first place to put the whole empire of Roumania in obedience to Rome, from which it has been separated this long while; further to give 200,000 marks of silver to those of the host, with food for one year for small and great; to send 10,000 men, horse and foot - many on foot as we shall devise and as many mounted-in his own ships, and at his own charges, to the land of Babylon, and keep them there for a year; and during his lifetime to keep, at his own charges, five hundred knights in the land overseass so that they may guard that land. Such is the covenant that your son made with us, and it was confirmed by oath, and charters with seals appended, and by King Philip of Germany who has your daughter to wife. This covenant we desire you to confirm."

Certes said the emperor, " this covenant is very onerous, and I do not see how effect can be given to it; nevertheless, you have done us such service, both to my son and to myself, that if we bestowed upon you the whole empire, you would have deserved it well." Many words were then spoken in this sense and that, but, in the end, the father confirmed the 'covenants, as his son had confirmed them, by oath and by charters with gold seals appended. These charters were delivered to the envoys. Then they took their leave of the Emperor Isaac, and went back to the host, and told the barons that they had fulfilled their mission.

ENTRY OF THE CRUSADERS INTO CONSTANTINOPLE - CORONATION OF THE YOUNG ALEXIUS

Then did the barons mount their horses, and led the young man, with great rejoicings, into the city, to his father; and the Greeks opened the gate to him, and received him with very much rejoicing and great feasting. The joy of the father and of the son was very great, because of a long time they had not seen one another, and because, by God's help and that of the pilgrims, they had passed from so great poverty and ruin to such high estate. Therefore the joy was great inside Constantinople; and also without, among the host of the pilgrims, because of the honour and victory that God had given them.

And on the morrow the emperor and his son also besought the counts and the barons, for God's sake, to go and quarter themselves on the other side of the straits, toward Estanor and Galata; for, if they quartered themselves in the city, it was to be feared that quarrels would ensue between them and the Greeks, and it might well chance that the city would be destroyed. And the counts and barons said that they had

48

already served him in so many ways that they would not now refuse any request of his. So they went and quartered themselves on the other side, and sojoumed there in peace and quiet, and with great store of good provisions.

Now you must know that many of those in the host went to see

Constantinople, and the rich palaces and great churches, of which there were many, and all the great wealth of the city-for never was there city that possessed so much. Of relics it does not behove me to speak, for at that day there were as many there as in all the rest of the world. Thus did the Greeks and French live in good fellowship in all things, both as regards trafficking and other matters.

By common consent of Franks and Greeks it was settled that the new emperor should be crowned on the feast of our Lord St. Peter (1st August 1203). So was it settled, and so it was done. He was crowned full worthily and with honour according to the use for Greek emperors at that time. Afterwards he began to pay the moneys due to the host; and such moneys were divided among the host, and each repaid what had been advanced in Venice for his passage.

ALEXIUS BEGS THE CRUSADERS TO PROLONG THEIR STAY

The new emperor went oft to see the barons in the camp, and did them great honour, as much as he could; and this was but fitting, seeing that they had served him right well. And one day he came to the camp, to see the barons privily in the quarters of Count Baldwin of Hainault and Flanders. Thither were summoned the Doge of Venice, and the great barons, and he spoke to them and said: " Lords, I am emperor by God's grace and yours, and you have done me the highest service that ever yet was done by any people to Christian man. Now be it known to you that there are folk enough who show me a fair seeming, and yet love me not; and the Greeks are full of despite because it is by your help that I have entered into my inheritance.

Now the term of your departure is nigh, and your fellowship with the Venetians is timed only to last till the feast of St. Michael. And within so short a term I cannot fulfil our covenant. Be it known to you therefore, that, if you abandon me, the Greeks hate me because of you: I shall losemy land, and they will kill me. But now do this thing that

49

I ask of you: remain here till March, and I will entertain your ships for one year from the feast of St. Michael, and bear the cost of the Venetians, and will give you such things as you may stand in need of till Easter. And within that term I shall have placed my land in such case that I cannot lose it again; and your covenant will be fulfilled, for I shall have paid such moneys as are due to you, obtaining them from all mi lands; and I shall be ready also with ships either to go with you myself, or to send others, as I have covenanted; and you will have the summer from end to end in which to carry on the war against the Saracens."

The barons thereupon said they would consult together apart; knowing full well that what the young man said was sooth, and that it would be better, both for the emperor and for themselves, to consent unto him. But they replied that they could not so consent save with the common agreement of the host, and that they would therefore lay the matter before the host, and then give such answer as might be devised. So the Emperor Alexius departed from them, and went back to Constantinople. And they remained in the camp and assembled a parliament the next day. To this parliament were summoned all the barons and the chieftains of the host, and of the knights the greater part; and in their hearing were repeated all the words that the emperor had spoken.

DEBATE AMONG THE CRUSADERS - DEATH OF MATTHEW OF MONTMORENCY

Then was there much discord in the host, as had been oft times before on the part of those who wished that the host should break up; for to them it seemed to be holding together too long. And the party that had raised the discord at Corfu reminded the others of their oaths, and said: " Give us ships as you swore to us, for we purpose to go to Syria."

And the others cried to them for pity and said: " Lords, for God's sake, let us not bring to naught the great honour that God has given us. If we go to Syria at this present, we shall come thither at the beginning of winter and so not be able to make war, and the Lord's work will thus remain undone. But if we wait till March, we shall leave this emperor in good estate, and go hence rich in goods and in food. Thus

50

shall we go to Syria, and over-run the land of Babylon. And the fleet will remain with us till Michaelmas, yes, and onwards from Michaelmas to Easter, seeing it will be unable to leave us because of the winter. So shall the land overseas fall into our hands."

Those who wished the host to be broken up, cared not for reasons good or bad so long as the host fell to pieces. But those who wished to keep the host together, wrought so effectually, with the help of God, that in the end the Venetians made a new covenant to maintain the fleet for a year, reckoning from Michaelmas, the Emperor Alexius paying them for so doing; and the pilgrims, on their side, made a new covenant to remain in the same fellowship as theretofore, and for the same term. Thus were peace and concord established in the host.

Then there befell a very great mischance in the host; for Matthew of Montmorency, who was one of the best knights in the kingdom of France, and of the most prized and most honoured, took to his bed for sickness, and his sickness so increased upon him that he died. And much dole was made for him, for great was the loss-one of the greatest that had befallen the host by any man's death. He was buried in a church of my Lord St. John, of the Hospital of Jerusalem.

PROGRESS OF THE YOUNG ALEXIUS THROUGH THE EMPIRE

Afterwards, by the advice of the Greeks and the French the Emperor Alexius issued from Constantinople, with a very great company, purposing to quiet the empire and subject it to his will. With him went a great part of the barons; and the others remained to guard the camp. The Marquis Boniface of Montferrat went with him, and Count Hugh of St. Paul, and Henry, brother to Count Baldwin of Flanders and Hainault, and James of Avesnes, and William of Champlitte, and Hugh of Colerni, and many others whom the book does not here mention by name. In the camp remained Count Baldwin of Flanders and Hainault, and Count Louis of Blois and Chartres, and the greater part of the pilgrims of lesser note.

And you must know that during this progress all the Greeks, on either side of the straits, came to the Emperor

51

Alexius, to do his will and commandment, and did him fealty and homage as to their lord-all except John, who was King of Wallachia and Bulgaria. This John was a Wallachian, who had rebelled against. his father and uncle, and had warred against them for twenty years, and had won from them so much land that he had become a very wealthy king. -And be it known to you, that of the land lying on the west side of the Straits of St. George, he had conquered very nearly the half. This John did not come to do the will of the emperor, nor to submit himself to him.

CONFLICT BETWEEN THE GREEKS AND LATINS IN CONSTANTINOPLE-BURNING OF THE CITY

While the Emperor Alexius was away on this progress, there befell a very grievous misadventure; for a conflict arose between the Greeks and the Latins who inhabited Constantinople, and of these last there were many. And certain people-who they were I know not-out of malice, set fire to the city; and the fire waxed so great and horrible that no man could put it out or abate it. And when the barons of the host, who were quartered on the other side of the port, saw this, they were sore grieved and filled with pity-seeing the great churches and the rich palaces melting and falling in, and the great streets filled with merchandise burning in the flames; but they could do nothing.

Thus did the fire prevail, and win across the port, even to the densest part of the city, and to the sea on the other side, quite near to the church of St. Sophia. It lasted two days and two nights, nor could it be put out by the hand of man. And the front of the fire, as it went flaming, was well over half a league broad. What was the damage then done, what the possessions and riches swallowed up, could no man tell-nor what the number of men and women and children who perished-for many were burned.

All the Latins, to whatever land they might belong, who were lodged in Constantinople, dared no longer to remain therein; but they took their wives and their children, and such of their possessions as they could save from the fire, and entered into boats and vessels, and passed over the port and came to the camp of the pilgrims. Nor were they few in number, for there were of them some fifteen thousand, small

52

and great; and afterwards it proved to be of advantage to the pilgrims that these should have crossed over to them. Thus was there division between the Greeks and the Franks; nor were they ever again as much at one as they had been before, for neither side knew on whom to cast the blame for the fire; and this rankled in men's hearts upon either side.

At that time did a thing befall whereby the barons and those of the host were greatly saddened; for the Abbot of Loos died, who was a holy man and a worthy, and had wished well to the host. He was a monk of the order of the Cistercians.

THE YOUNG ALEXIUS RETURNS TO CONSTANTINOPLIZHE FAILS IN HIS PROMISES TO THE CRUSADERS

The Emperor Alexius remained for a long time on progress, till St. Martin's Day, and then he returned to Constantinople. Great was the joy at his home-coming, and the Greeks and ladies of Constantinople went out to meet their friends in great cavalcades, and the pilgrims went out to meet their friends, and had great joy of them. So did the emperor re-enter Constantinople and the palace of Blachernae; and the Marquis of Montferrat and the other barons returned to the camp.

The emperor, who had managed his affairs right well and thought he had now the upper hand, was filled with arrogance towards the barons and those who had done so much for him, and never came to see them in the camp, as he had done aforetime. And they sent to him and begged him to pay them the moneys due, as he had covenanted. But he led them on from delay to delay, making them, at one time and another, payments small and poor; and in the end the payments ceased and came to naught.

The Marquis Boniface of Montferrat, who had done more for him than any other, and stood better in his regard, went to him oftentimes, and showed him what great services the Crusaders had rendered him, and that greater services had never been rendered to any one. And the emperor still entertained them with delays, and never carried out such things as he had promised, so that at last they saw and knew clearly that his intent was wholly evil.

Then the barons of the host held a parliament with the

53

Doge of Venice, and they said that they now knew that the emperor would fulfil no covenant, nor ever speak sooth to them; and they decided to send good envoys to demand the fulfilment of their covenant, and to show what services they had done him; and if he would now do what was required, they were to be satisfied; but, if not, they were to defy him, and right well might he rest assured that the barons would by all means recover their due.

THE CRUSADERS DEFY THE EMPERORS

For this embassy were chosen Conon of Béthune and Geoffry of Villehardouin, the Marshal of Champagne, and Miles the Brabant of Provins; and the Doge also sent three chief men of his council. So these envoys mounted their horses, and, with swords girt, rode together till they came to the palace of Blachernae. And be it known to you that, by reason of the treachery of the Greeks, they went in great peril, and on a hard adventure.

They dismounted at the gate and entered the palace, and found the Emperor Alexius and the Emperor Isaac seated on two thrones, side by side. And near them was seated the empress, who was the wife of the father, and stepmother of the son, and sister to the King of Hungary-a lady both fair and good. And there were with them a great company of people of note and rank, so that well did the court seem the court of a rich and mighty prince.

By desire of the other envoys Conon of Béthune, who was very wise and eloquent of speech, acted as spokesman: "Sire, we have come to thee on the part of the barons of the host and of the Doge of Venice. They would put thee in mind of the great service they have done to thee-a service known to the people and manifest to all men. Thou hast swom, thou and thy father, to fulfil the promised covenants, and they have your charters in hand. But you have not fulfilled those covenants well, as you should have done. Many times have they called upon you to do so, and now again we call upon you, in the presence of all your barons, to fulfil the covenants that are between you and them. Should you do so, it shall be well. If not, be it known to you that from this day forth they will not hold you as lord or friend, but will endeavour to obtain their due by all the means in their

54

Power. And of this they now give you warning, seeing that they would not injure you, nor any one, without first defiance given; for never have they acted treacherously, nor in their land is it customary to do so. You have heard what we have said. It is for you to take counsel thereon according to your pleasure."

Much were the Greeks amazed and greatly outraged by this open defiance; and they said that never had any one been so hardy as to dare defy the Emperor of Constantinople in his own hall. Very evil were the looks now cast on the envoys by the Emperor Alexius and by all the Greeks, who aforetime were wont to regard them very favourably.

Great was the tumult there within, and the envoys turned about and came to the gate and mounted their horses. When they got outside the gate, there was not one of them but felt glad at heart; nor is that to be marvelled at, for they had escaped from very great peril, and it held to very little that they were not all killed or taken. So they returned to the camp, and told the barons how they had fared.

THE WAR BEGINS - THE GREEKS ENDEAVOUR TO SET FIRE TO THE FLEET OF THE CRUSADERS

Thus did the war begin; and each side did to the other as much harm as they could, by sea and by land. The Franks and the Greeks fought often; but never did they fight, let God be praised therefor I that the Greeks did not lose more than the Franks. So the war lasted a long space, till the heart of the winter.

Then the Greeks bethought themselves of a very great device, for they took seven large ships, and filled them full of big logs, and shavings, and tow, and resin, and barrels, and then waited until such time as the wind should blow strongly from their side of the straits. And one night, at midnight, they set fire to the ships, and unfurled their sails to the wind. And the flames blazed up high, so that it seemed as if the whole world were a-fire. Thus did the burning ships come towards the fleet of the pilgrims; and a great cry arose in the host, and all sprang to arms on every side. The Venetians ran to their ships, and so did all those who had ships in possession, and they began to draw them away out of the flames very vigorously.

55

And to this bears witness Geoffry the Marshal of Champagne, who dictates this work, that never did people help themselves better at sea than the Venetians did that night; for they sprang into the galleys and boats belonging to the ships, and seized upon the fire ships, all burning as they were, with hooks, and dragged them by main force before their enemies, outside the port, and set them into the current of the straits, and left them to go burning down the straits. So many of the Greeks had come down to the shore that they were without end and innumerable, and their cries were so great that it seemed as if the earth and sea would melt together. They got into barges and boats, and shot at those on our side who were battling with the flames, so that some were wounded.

All the knights of the host, as soon as they heard the clamour, armed themselves; and the battalions marched out into the plain, each according to the order in which they had been quartered, for they feared lest the Greeks should also attack them on land.

They endured thus in labour and anguish till daylight; but by God's help those on our side lost nothing, save a Pisan ship, which was full of merchandise, and was burned with fire. Deadly was the peril in which we stood that night, for if the fleet had been consumed, all would have been lost, and we should never have been able to get away by land or sea. Such was the guerdon which the Emperor Alexius would have bestowed upon us in return for our services.

MOURZUPHLES USURPS THE EMPIRE - ISAAC DIES, AND THE YOUNG ALEXIUS IS STRANGLED

Then the Greeks, being thus embroiled with the Franks, saw that there was no hope of peace; so they privily took counsel together to betray their lord. Now there was a Greek who stood higher in his favour than all others, and had done more to make him embroil himself with the Franks than any other. This Greek was named Mourzuphles.

With the advice and consent of the others, one night towards midnight, when the Emperor Alexius was asleep in his chamber, those who ought to have been guarding him and specially Mourzuphles-took him in his bed and threw him into a dungeon in prison. Then Mourzuphles assumed

56

the scarlet buskins with the help and by the counsel of the other Greeks (January 1204). So he made himself emperor. Afterwards they crowned him at St. Sophia. Now see if. ever people were guilty of such horrible treachery!

When the Emperor Isaac heard that his son was taken and Mourzuphles crowned, great fear came upon him, and he fell into a sickness that lasted no long time. So he died. And the Emperor Mourzuphles caused the son, whom he had in prison, to be poisoned two or three times; but it did not please God that he should thus die. Afterwards the emperor went and strangled him, and when he had strangled him, he caused it to be reported everywhere that he had died a natural death, and had him mourned for, and buried honourably and as an emperor, and made great show of grief.

But murder cannot be hid. Soon was it clearly known, both to the Greeks and to the French, that this murder had been committed, as has just been told to you. Then did the barons of the host and the Doge of Venice assemble in parliament, and with them met the bishops and the clergy. And all the clergy, including those who had powers from the Pope, showed to the barons and to the pilgrims that any one guilty of such a murder had no right to hold lands, and that those who consented thereto were abettors of the murder; and beyond all this, that the Greeks had withdrawn themselves from obedience to Rome. "Wherefore we tell you," said the clergy, " that this war is lawful and just, and that if you have a right intention in conquering this land, to bring it into the Roman obedience, all those who die after confession shall have part in the indulgence granted by the Pope." And you must know that by this the barons and pilgrims were greatly comforted.

THE CRUSADERS CONTINUE THE WAR - DEFEAT OF MOURZUPHLES

Dire was the war between the Franks and the Greeks, for it abated not, but rather increased and waxed fiercer, so that few were the days on which there was not fighting by sea or land. Then Henry, the brother of Count Baldwin of Flanders rode forth, and took with him a great part of the good men in the host. With him went James of Avesnes, and Baldwin of Beauvoir, Odo of Champagne of Champlitte,

William his brother, and the people of their country. They started at vesper time and rode all night, and on the morrow, when it was full day, they came to a good city, called Phile, and took it; and they had great gain, beasts, and prisoners, and clothing, and food, which they sent in boats down the straits to the camp, for the city lies on the sea of Russia.

So they sojourned two days in that city, with food in great plenty, enough and to spare. The third day they departed with the beasts and the booty, and rode back towards the camp. Now the Emperor Mourzuphles heard tell how they had issued from the camp, and he left Constantinople by night, with a great part of his people, and set himself in ambush at a place by which they must needs pass. And he watched them pass with their beasts and their booty, each division, the one after the other, till it came to the rearguard. The rear-guard was under the command of Henry, the brother of Count Baldwin of Flanders, and formed of his people, and the Emperor Mourzuphles fell upon them at the entrance to a wood; whereupon they turned against him. Very fiercely did the battle rage there.

By God's help the Emperor Mourzuphles was discomfited, and came near to being taken captive; and he lost his imperial banner and an Eikon that was home before him, in which he and the other Greeks had great confidence-it was an ikon that figured our Lady-and he lost at least twenty knights of the best people that he had. Thus was discomfited the Emperor Mourzuphles, as you have just heard and fiercely did the war rage between him and the Franks; and by this time a great part of the winter had already passed, and it was near Candlemas (2nd February 1204), and Lent was approaching.

OF THE PILGRIMS WHO HAD GONE TO SYRIA

Now we will leave off speaking of the host before Constantinople, and speak of those who sailed from other ports than Venice, and of the ships of Flanders that had sojourned during the winter at Marseilles, and had all gone over in the summer to the land of Syria; and these were far more in number than the host before Constantinople. Listen now, and you shall hear what a great mischance it was that they

had not joined themselves to the host, for in that case would Christendom have been for ever exalted. But because of their sins, God would not so have it, for some died of the sickness of the land, and some turned back to their own homes. Nor did they perform any great deeds, or achieve aught of good, in the land overseass

And there started also a company of very good men to go to Antioch, to join Boemond, prince of Antioch and Count of Tripoli, who was at war with King Leon, the lord of the Armenians. This company was going to the prince to be in his pay; and the Turks of the land knew of it, and made an ambuscade there where the men of the company needs must pass. And they came thither, and fought, and the Franks were discomfited, so that not one escaped that was not killed or taken.

There were slain Villain of Neuilly, who was one of the best knights in the world, and Giles of Trasegnies, and many others; and were taken Bernard of Moreuil, and Renaud of Dampierre, and John of Villers, and William of Neuilly. And you must know that eightty knights were in this company, and every one was either killed or taken. And well does this book bear witness, that of those who avoided the host of Venice, there was not one but suffered harm or shame. He therefore must be accounted wise who holds to the better course.

AGREEMENT BETWEEN THE FRANKS AND VENETIANS BEFORE ATTACKING CONSTANTINOPLE

Now let us leave speaking of those who avoided the host, and speak of those before Constantinople. Well had these prepared all their engines, and mounted their petraries, and mangonels on the ships and on the transports, and got ready all such engines of war as are needful for the taking of a city, and raised ladders from the yards and masts of the vessels, so high that they were a marvel to behold.* *[note: This passage is obscure in the original.]* And when the Greeks saw this, they began, on their side, to strengthen the defences of the city which was enclosed with high walls and high towers. Nor was any tower so high that they did not raise thereon two or three stages of wood to heighten it still more. Never was city so well fortified.

59

Thus did the Greeks and the Franks bestir themselves on the one side and the other during the greater part of Lent.

Then those of the host spoke together, and took counsel what they should do. Much was advanced this way and that, but in the end, they devised that if God granted them entry into the city by force, all the booty taken was to be brought together, and fittingly distributed; and further, if the city fell into their power, six men should be taken from among the Franks, and six from among the Venetians, and these twelve should swear, on holy relics, to elect as emperor the man who, as they deemed, would rule with most profit to the land. And whosoever was thus elected emperor, would have one quarter of whatever was captured, whether within the city or without, and moreover would possess the palace of Bucoleon and that of Blachernae; and the remaining three parts would be divided into two, and one of the halves awarded to the Venetians and the other to those of the host.

And there should be taken twelve of the wisest and most experienced men among the host of the pilgrims, and twelve among the Venetians, and those twenty-four would divide fiefs and honours, and appoint the service to be done therefor to the emperor.

This covenant was made sure and sworn to on the one side and the other b' the Franks and the Venetians; with provision that at the end of March, a year thence, any who so desired might depart hence and go their way, but that those who remained in the land would be held to the service of the emperor in such mariner as might be ordained. Thus was the covenant devised and made sure; and such as should not observe it were excommunicated by the clergy.

ATTACK OF THE CRUSADERS REPULSED - THEY MAKE READY FOR ANOTHER ASSAULT

The fleet was very well prepared and armed, and provisions were got together for the pilgrims. On the Thursday after mid-Lent (8th April 1204), all entered into the vessels, and put their horses into the transports. Each division had its own ships, and all were ranged side by side; and the ships were separated from the galleys and transports. A marvellous sight it was to see; and well does this book bear

60

witness that the attack, as it had been devised, extended over full half a French league.

On the Friday morning the ships and the galleys and the other vessels drew near to the city in due order, and then began an assault most fell and fierce. In many places the pilgrims landed and went up to the walls, and in many places the scaling ladders on the ships approached so close, that those on the towers and on the walls and those on the ladders crossed lances, hand to hand. Thus lasted the assault, in more than a hundred places, very fierce, and very dour, and very proud, till near upon the hour of nones.

But, for our sins, the pilgrims were repulsed in that assault, and those who had landed from the galleys and transports were driven back into them by main force. And you must know that on that day those of the host lost more than the Greeks, and much were the Greeks rejoiced thereat. And some there were who drew back from the assault, with the ships in which they were. And some remained with their ships at anchor so near to the city that from either side they shot at one another with petraries and mangonels.

Then, at vesper time, those of the host and the Doge of Venice called together a parliament, and assembled in a church on the other side of the straits-on the side where they had been quartered. There were many opinions given and discussed; and much were those of the host moved for the mischief that had that day befallen them. And many advised that they should attack the city on another side the side where it was not so well fortified. But the Venetians, who had fuller knowledge of the sea, said that if they went to that other side, the current would carry them down the straits, and that they would be unable to stop their ships. And you must know that there were those who would have been well pleased if the current had home them down the straits, or the wind, they cared not whither, so long -as they left that land behind, and went on their way. Nor is this to be wondered at, for they were in sore peril.

Enough was there spoken, this way and in that; but the conclusion of their deliberation was this: that they would repair and refit on the following day, which was Saturday, and during the whole of Sunday, and that on the Monday they would return to the assault; and they devised further that the ships that carried the scaling ladders should be

61

bound together, two and two, so that two ships should be in case to attack one tower; for they had perceived that day how only one ship had attacked each tower, and that this had been too heavy a task for the ship, seeing that those in the tower were more in number than those on the ladder. For this reason was it well seen that two ships would attack each tower with greater effect than one. As had been settled, so was it done, and they waited thus during the Saturday and Sunday.

THE CRUSADERS TAKE A PART OF THE CITY

Before the assault the Emperor Mourzuphles had come to encamp, with all his power, in an open space, and had there pitched his scarlet tents. Thus matters remained till the Monday morning, when those on the ships, transports, and galleys were all armed. And those of the city stood in much less fear of them than they did at the beginning, and were in such good spirits that on the walls and towers you could see nothing but people. Then began an assault proud and marvellous, and every ship went straight before it to the attack. The noise of the battle was so great that it seemed to read the earth.

Thus did the assault last for a long while, till our Lord raised a wind called Boreas which drove the ships and vessels further up on to the shore. And two ships that were bound together, of which the one was called the Pilgrim and the other the *Paradise,* approached so near to a tower, the one on the one side and the other on the other-so as God and the wind drove them-that the ladder of the Pilgrim joined on to the tower. Immediately a Venetian, and a knight of France, whose name was Andrew of Urboise, entered into the tower, and other people benan to enter after them, and those in the tower were discomfited and fled.*

> *[NOTE [pp. 61-63]: I should like to quote here another feat of arms related by **Robert of Clari**, one of those feats that serve to explain how the Crusaders obtained mastery - the mastery of perfect fearlessness - over the Greeks. Robert of Clari, then, relates how a small body of the besiegers, ten knights and nine sergeants, had come before a postem which had been newly bricked up.-*

> *"Now there was there a clerk, Aleaume of Clari by name, who had shown his courage whenever there was need, and was always first in any assault at which he might be present; and when the tower of Galata was taken, this same clerk had performed more deeds of prowess with his body, man for man, than any one in the host, save only the Lord Peter of Bracuel; for the Lord Peter it was who surpassed all others, whether of high or low degree, so that there was none other that performed such feats of arms, or acts of prowess with his body, as the Lord Peter of Bracuel. So when they came to the postern they began to hew and pick at it very hardily; but the bolts flew at them so thick, and so many stones were hurled at them from the wall, that it seemed as if they would be buried beneath the stones-sucb was the mass of quarries and stones thrown from above. And those who were below held up targes and shields to cover those who were picking and hewing underneath; and those above threw down pots of boiling pitch, and Greek fire, and large rocks, so that it was one of God's miracles that the assailants were not utterly confounded; for my Lord Peter and his men suffered more than enough of blows and grievous danger. However, so did they hack at the postern, both above and below, with their axes and good swords, that they made a great bole therein; and when the postern was broken through, they all swarmed to the aperture, but saw so many people above and below, that it seemed as if half the world were there, and they dared not be so bold as to enter.*

> *"Now when Aleaume, the clerk, saw that no one dared to go in, be*

sprang forward, and said that go in he would. And there was there present a knight, a brother to the clerk (the knight's name was Robert ofClari),who-forbade him,and said he should not go in. And the clerk said he would, and scrambled in on his hands and feet. And when the knight saw this, he took hold upon him, by the foot, and began to drag him back. But in his brother's despite, and whether his brother would or not, the clerk went in. And when he was within, many were the Greeks who ran upon him, and those on the walls cast big stones upon him. And the clerk drew his knife, and ran at them; and he drave them before him as if they had been cattle, and cried to those who were without, to the Lord Peter of Amiens and his folk, 'Sire, come in boldly, I see that they are falling back discomfited and flying.' When my Lord Peter heard this, he and his people who were without, they entered in; and there were no more than ten knights with him, but there were some sixty sergeants, and they were all on foot. And when those who were on the wall at that place saw them, they had such fear that they did not dare to remain there, but avoided a great space on the wall, and fled helter-skelter.

"Now the Emperor Mourzuphles, the traitor, was near by, at less than a stone's throw of distance, and he caused the silver horns to be sounded, and the cymbals, and a great noise to be made. And when he saw my Lord Peter, and his people, who bad entered in on foot, he made a great show of falling upon them, and spurring forward, came about half-way to where they stood. But mv Lord Peter, when he saw him coming, began to encourage his people, and to say: 'Now, Lord God, grant that we may do well, and the battle is ours. Here comes the emperor! Let no one dare to think of retreat, but each bethink himself to do well' Then Mourzuphles, seeing that they would in no wise give way, stayed where he was, and then turned back to his tents."

After this, according to Robert of Clari, Lord Peter's men break open a gate, and.the Crusaders enter into the city. See Li Estoires de chiaus qus conquisent Constantinoble. de Robert de Clari en aminois, chevalier, *pp. 60-62. The volume in the British Museum is undated, and there is this note in the catalogue, " No more printed." The volume itself is noteless, though there are printed marks here and there which would suggest that notes were intended. The Chronicle of Robert of Clari win also be found in Hopf 's* Chroniques Gréco-romanes inédites ou peu connues, *etc., pp. 1-85, Berlin, 1873.]*

When the knights see this, who are in the transports, they land, and raise their ladders against the wall, and scale the top of the wall by main force, and so take four of the towers. And all begin to leap out of the ships and transports and galleys, helter-skelter, each as best he can; and they break in some three of the gates and enter in; and they draw the horses out of the transports; and the knights mount and ride straight to the quarters of the Emperor Mourzuphles. He had his battalions arrayed before his tents, and when his men see the mounted knights coming, they lose heart and fly; and so goes the emperor flying through the streets to the castle of Bucoleon.

Then might you have seen the Greeks beaten down; and horses and palfreys captured, and mules, and other booty. Of killed and wounded there was neither end nor measure. A great part of the Greek lords had fled towards the gate of

Blachernae. And vesper-time was already past, and those of the host were wear of the battle and of the slaying,. And they began to assemble in a great open space that was in Constantinople, and decided that they would take up their quarters near the walls and towers they had captured. Never had they thought that in a whole month they should be able to take the city, with its great churches, and great palaces, and the people that were in it.

FLIGHT OF MOURZUPHLES - SECOND FIRE IN CONSTANTINOPLE

As they had settled, so was it done, and they encamped before the walls and before the towers by their ships. Count Baldwin of Flanders and Hainault quartered himself in the scarlet tents that the Emperor Mourzuphles had left standing, and Henry his brother before the palace of Blachernae; and Boniface, Marquis of Montferrat, he and his men, towards the thickest part of the city. So were the host encamped as you have heard, and Constantinople taken on the Monday after Palm Sunday (12th April 1204).

Now Count Louis of Blois and Chartres had languished all the winter with a q ' uartan fever, and could not bear his armour. And you must know that this was a great misfor-

tune to the host, seeing he was a good knight of his body; and he lay in one of the transports.

Thus did those of the host, who were very weary, rest that night. But the Emperor Mourzuphles rested not, for he assembled all his people, and said he would go and attack the Franks. Nevertheless he did not do as he had said, for he rode along other streets, as far as he could from those held by the host, and came to a gate which is called the Golden Gate, whereby he escaped, and avoided the city; and afterwards all who could fled also. And of all this those of the host knew nothing.

During that night, towards the quarters of Boniface Marquis of Montferrat, certain people, whose names are unknown to me, being in fear lest the Greeks should attack them, set fire to the buildings between themselves and the Greeks. And the city began to take fire, and to burn very direfully; and it burned all that night and all the next day, till vesper-time. And this was the third fire there had been in Constantinople since the Franks arrived in the land; and more houses had been burned in the city than there are houses in any three of the greatest cities in the kingdom of France.

That night passed and the next day came, which was a Tuesday morning (13th April 1204); and all armed themselves throughout the host, both knights and sergeants, and each repaired to his post. Then they issued from their quarters, and thought to find a sorer battle than the day before, for no word had come to them that the emperor had fled during the night. But they found none to oppose them.

THE CRUSADERS OCCUPY THE CITY

The Marquis Boniface of Montferrat rode all along the shore to the palace of Bucoleon, and when he arrived there it surrendered, on condition that the lives of all therein should be spared. At Bucoleon were found the larger number of the great ladies who had fled to the castle, for there were found the sister *[Agnes, sister of Philip Augustus, married successively to Alexius II., to Andronicus, and to Theodore Branas]* of the King of France, who had been empress, and the sister *[Margaret, sister of Emeric, King of Hungary, married to the Emperor Isaac, and afterwards to the Marquis of Montferrat.]* of the King of Hungary, who

65

had also been empress, and other ladies very many. Of the treasure that was found in that palace I cannot well speak, for there was so much that it was beyond end or counting.

At the same time that this palace was surrendered to the Marquis Boniface of Montferrat, did the palace of Blachernae surrender to Henry, the brother of

Count Baldwin of Flanders, on condition that no hurt should be done to the bodies of those who were therein. There too was found much treasure, not less than in the palace of Bucoleon. Each garrisoned with his own people the castle that had been surrendered to him, and set a auard over the treasure. And the other people, spread abroad throughout the city, also gained much booty. The booty gained was so great that none could tell you the end of it: gold and silver, and vessels and precious stones, and samite, and cloth of silk, and robes vair and grey, and ermine, and every choicest thing found upon the earth. And well does Geoffry of Villehardouin the Marshal of Champagne, bear witness, that never, since the world was created, had so much booty been won in any city.

Every one took quarters where he pleased and of lodgings there was no stint. So the host of the pilgrims and of the Venetians found quarters, and greatly did they rejoice and give thanks because of the victory God had vouchsafed to them-for those who before had been poor were now in wealth and luxury. Thus they celebrated Palm Sunday and the Easter Day following (25th April 1204) in the joy and honour that God had bestowed upon them. And well miaht they praise our Lord, since in all the host there were no more than twenty thousand armed men, one with another, and with the help of God they had conquered four hundred thousand men, or more, and in the strongest city in all the world - yea, a great city - and very well fortified.

DIVISION OF THE SPOIL

Then was it proclaimed throughout the host by the Marquis Boniface of Montferrat, who was lord of the host, and by the barons, and by the Doge of Venice, that all the booty should be collected and brou-ht together, as had been covenanted under oath and pain of excommunication. Three churches were appointed for the receiving of the

66

spoils, and guards were set to have them in charge, both Franks and Venetians, the most upright that could be found.

Then each began to bring in such booty as he had taken, and to collect it together. And some brought in loyally, and some in evil sort, because covetousness, which is the root of all evil, let and hindered them. So from that time forth the covetous began to keep things back, and our Lord began to love them less. Ah God! how loyally they had borne themselves up to now! And well had the Lord God shown them that in all things He was ready to honour and exalt them above all people. But full oft do the good suffer for the sins of the wicked.

The spoils and booty were collected together, and you must know that all was not brought into the common stock, for not a few kept thin-s back, maugre the excommunication of the Pope. That which was brought to the churches was collected together and divided, in equal parts, between the Franks and the Venetians, according to the sworn covenant. And you must know further that the pilgrims, after the division had been made, paid out of their share fifty thousand marks of silver to the Venetians, and then divided at least one hundred thousand marks between themselves, among their own people. And shall I tell you in what wise? Two sergeants on foot counted as one mounted, and two sergeants mounted as one knight. And you must know that no man received more, either on account of his rank or because of his deeds, than that which had been so settled and orderedsave in so far as he may have stolen it.

And as to theft, and those who were convicted thereof, you must know that stem justice was meted out to such as were found guilty, and not a few were hung. The Count of St. Paul hung one of his knights, who had kept back certain spoils, with his shield to his neck; but many there were, both great and small, who kept back part of the spoils, and it was never known. Well may you be assured that the spoil wa- very great, for if it had not been for what was stolet- and for the part given to the Venetians, there would if have been at least four hundred thousand marks of silver and at least ten thousand horses-one with another. Thus were divided the spoils of Constantinople, as you have heard.

67

BALDWIN, COUNT OF FLANDERS, ELECTED EMPEROR

Then a parliament assembled, and the commons of the host declared that an emperor must be elected, as had been settled aforetime. And they parliamented so long that the matter was adjourned to another day, and on that day would they choose the twelve electors who were to make the election. Nor was it possible that there should be lack of candidates, or of men covetous, seeing that so great an honour was in question as the imperial throne of Constantinople. But the greatest discord that arose was the discord concerning Count Baldwin of Flanders and Hainault and the Marquis Boniface of Montferrat; for all the people said that either of those two should be elected.

And when the chief men of the host saw that all held either for Count Baldwin or for the Marquis of Montferrat, they conferred together and said: " Lords, if we elect one of these two great men, the other will be so filled with envy that he will take away with him all his people. And then the land that we have won may be lost, just as the land of Jerusalem came nigh to be lost when, after it had been conquered, Godfrey of Bouillon was elected king, and the Count of St. Giles became so fulfilled with envy that he enticed the other barons, and whomsoever he could, to abandon the host. Then did many people depart, and there remained so few that, if God had not sustained them, the land of Jerusalem wouldhavebeenlost. Letusthereforebewarelestthesame mischance befall us also, and rather bethink ourselves how we may keep both these lords in the host. Let the one on whom God shall bestow the empire so devise that the other is well content; let him grant to that other all the land on the further side of the straits, towards Turkey, and the Isle of Greece, and that other shall be his liegeman. Thus shall we keep both lords in the host."

As had been proposed, so was it settled, and both consented right willingly. Then came the day for the parliament, and the parliament assembled. And the twelve electors were chosen, six on one side and six on the other; and they swore on holy relics to elect, duly, and in good faith, whomsoever would best meet the needs of the host, and bear rule over the empire most worthily.

68

Thus were the twelve chosen, and a day appointed for the election of the emperor; and on the appointed day the twelve electors met at a rich palace, one of the fairest in the world, where the Doge of Venice had his quarters. Great and marvellous was the concourse, for every one wished to see who should be elected. Then were the twelve electors called, and set in a very rich chapel within the palace, and the door was shut, so that no one remained with them. The barons and knights stayed without in a great palace.

The council lasted till they were agreed; and by consent' of all they appointed Nevelon, Bishop of Soissons, who was one of the twelve, to act as spokesman. Then they came out to the place where all the barons were assembled, and the Doge of Venice. Now you must know that many set eyes upon them, to know how the election had turned. And the bishop, lifting up his voice-while all listened intentlyspoke as he had been charged, and said: " Lords, we are agreed, let God be thanked! upon the choice of an emperor; and you have all sworn that he whom we shall elect as ern,,)eror shall be held by you to be emperor indeed, and that it any one gainsay him, you will be his helpers. And we name him now at the self-same hour when God was born, THE COUNT BALDWIN OF FLANDERS AND HAINAULT! "

A cry of joy was raised in the palace, and they bore the count out of the palace, and the Marquis Boniface of Montferrat bore him on one side to the church, and showed him all the honour he could. So was the Count Baldwin of Flanders and Hainault elected emperor, and a day appointed for his coronation, three weeks after Easter (16th May 1204). And you must know that many a rich robe was made for the coronation; nor did they want for the wherewithal.

BONIFACE WEDS ISAAC'S WIDOW, AND AFTER BALDWIN'S CORONATION OBTAINS THE KINGDOM OF SALONIKA

Before the time appointed for the coronation, the Marquis Boniface of Montferrat espoused the empress who had been the wife of the Emperor Isaac, and was sister to the King of Hungary. And within that time also did one of the most noble barons of the host, who bore the name of Odo of Champlitte of Champagne, make an end and die. Much was he mourned and bewept by William his brother, and by his

69

other friends; and he was buried in the church of the Apostles with great honour.

The time for the coronation drew near, and the Emperor Baldwin was crowned with great joy and great honour in the church of St. Sophia, in the year of the Incarnation of Jesus Christ one thousand twelve hundred and four. Of the rejoicings and feasting there is no need to speak further, for the barons and knights did all they could; and the Marquis Boniface of Montferrat and Count Louis of Blois and Chartres did homage to the emperor as their lord. After the great rejoicings and ceremonies of the coronation, he was taken in great pomp, and with a great procession, to the rich palace of Bucoleon. And when the feastings were over he began to discuss his affairs.

Boniface the Marquis of Montferrat called upon him to carry out the covenant made, and give him, as he was bound to do, the land on the other side of the straits towards Turkey and the Isle of Greece. And the emperor acknowledged that he was bound so to do, and said he would do it right willingly. And when the Marquis of Montferrat saw that the emperor was willing to carry out this covenant so debonairly, he besought him, in exchange for this land, to bestow upon him the kingdom of Salonika, because it lay near the land of the King of Hungary, whose sister he had taken to wife.

Much was this matter debated in various ways; but in the end the emperor granted the land of Salonika to the marquis, and the marquis did homage therefor. And at this there was much joy thr oughout , the host, because the marquis was one of the knights most highly prized in all the world, and one whom the knights most loved, inasmuch as no one dealt with them more liberally than he. Thus the marquis remained in the land, as you have heard.

BALDWIN MARCHES AGAINST MOURZUPHLES

The Emperor Mourzuphles had not yet removed more than four days' journey
from Constantinople; and he had taken with him the empress who had been
the wife of the Emperor Alexius, who aforetime had fled, and his daughter.
This Emperor Alexius was in a city called Messinopolis, with all his people,
and still held a great part of the land. And at that

70

time the men of note in Greece departed, and a large number passed over the
straits towards Turkey; and each one, for his own advantage, made himself
master of such lands as he could lay hands upon; and the same thing
happened also throughout the other parts of the empire.

The Emperor Mourzuphles made no long tarrying before he took a city which
had surrendered to my lord the Emperor Baldwin, a city called Tchorlu. So he
took it and sacked it, and seized whatever he found there. When the news
thereof came to the Emperor Baldwin, he took counsel with the barons, and
with the Doge of Venice, and they agreed to this, that he should issue forth,
with all his host, to make conquest of the land, and leave a garrison in
Constantinople to keep it sure, seeing that the city had been newly taken and
was peopled with the Greeks.

So did they decide, and the host was called together, and decision made as to
who should remain in Constantinople, and who should go in the host with the
Emperor Baldwin. In Constantinople remained Count Louis of Blois and
Chartres, who had been sick, and was not yet recovered, and the Doge of
Venice. And Conon of Béthune remained in the palaces of Blachemoe and
Bucoleon to keep the city; and with him Geoffry the Marshal of Champagne,
and Miles the Brabant of Provins, and Manasses of l'Isle, and all their people.
All the rest made ready to go in the host with the emperor.

Before the Emperor Baldwin left Constantinople, his brother Henry departed
thence, by his command, with a hundred very good knights; and he rode from
city to city, and in every city to which he came the people swore fealty to the
emperor. So he fared forward till he came to Adrianople, which was a good
city, and wealthy; and those of the city received him right willingly and swore
fealty to the emperor. Then he lodged in the city, he and his people, and
sojourned there till the Emperor Baldwin came thither.

MOURZUPHLES TAKES REFUGE WITH ALEXIUS, THE
BROTHER OF ISAAC, WHO PUTS OUT HIS EYES

The Emperor Mourzuphles, when he heard that they thus advanced against him, did not dare to abide their coming, but remained always two or three days' march in advance.

71

So he fared forward till he came near Messinopolis, where the Emperor Alexius was sojourning, and he sent on messengers, telling Alexius that he would give him help, and do all his behests. And the Emperor Alexius answered that he should be as welcome as if he were his own son, and that he would give him his daughter to wife, and make of him his son. So the Emperor Mourzuphles encamped before Messinopolis, and pitched his tents and pavilions, and Alexius was quartere within the city. So they conferred together, and Alexius gave him his daughter to wife, and they entered into alliance, and said they should be as one.

They sojourned thus for I know not how many days, the one in the camp and the other in the city, and then did the Emperor Alexius invite the Emperor MourzupWes to come and eat with him, and to go with him to the baths. So were matters settled. The Emperor Mourzuphles came privately, and with few people, and when he was within the house, the Emperor Alexius called him into a privy chamber, and had him thrown on to the ground, and the eyes drawn out of his head. And this was done in such treacherous wise as you have heard. Now say whether this people, who wrought such cruelty one to another, were fit to have lands in possession I And when the host of the Emperor Mourzuphles heard what had been done, they scattered, and fled this way and that; and some joined themselves to the Emperor Alexius, and obeyed him as their lord, and remained with him.

BALDWIN MARCHES AGAINST ALEXIUS-HE IS JOINED BY BONIFACE

Then the Emperor Baldwin moved from Constantinople, with all his host, and rode forward till he came to Adrianople. There he found Henry his brother, and the men with him. All the people whithersoever the emperor passed, came to him, and put themselves at his mercy and under his rule. And while they were at Adrianople, they heard the news that the Emperor Alexius had pulled out the eyes of the Emperor Mourzuphles. Of this there was much talk among them; and well did all say that those who betrayed one another so disloyally and treacherously had no right to hold land in possession.

Then was the Emperor Baldwin minded to ride straight to

72

Messinopolis, where the Emperor Alexius was. And the Greeks of Adrianople besought him, as their lord, to leave a garrison in their city because of Johannizza, King of Wallachia and Bulgaria, who ofttimes made war upon them. And the' Emperor Baldwin left there Eustace of Saubruic, who was a knight of Flanders, very worthy and very valiant, together with forty right good knights, and a hundred mounted sergeants.

So departed the Emperor Baldwin from Adrianople, and rode towards Messinopolis, where he thought to find the Emperor Alexius. All the people of the lands through which he passed put themselves under his rule and at his mercyand when the Emperor Alexius saw this, he avoided Messl-' nopolis and fled. And the Emperor Baldwin rode on till he came before Messinopolis; and those of the city went out to meet him and surrendered the city to his commandment.

Then the Emperor Baldwin said he would sojourn there, wafting for the arrival of Boniface, Marquis of Montferrat, who had not yet joined the host, seeing he could not move as fast as the emperor, because he was bringing with him the empress, his wife. However, he also rode forward till he came to Messinopolis, by the river, and there encamped, and pitched his tents and pavilions. And on the morrow he went to speak to the Emperor Baldwin, and to see him, and reminded him of his promise.

"Sire," said he, "tidings have come to me from Salonika that the people of the land would have me know that they are ready to receive me willingly as their lord. And I am your liegeman, and hold the land from you. Therefore, I pray you, let me go thither; and when I am in possession of my land and of my city, I will bring you out such supplies as you may need, and come ready prepared to do your behests. But do not go and ruin my land. Let us rather, if it so pleases you, march against Johannizz', the King of Wallachia and Bulgaria, who holds a great part of the land wrongfully."

RUPTURE BETWEEN BALDWIN AND B0NIFACE - THE ONE MARCHES ON SALONIKA, THE OTHER ON DEMOTICA

I know not by whose counsel it was that the emperor replied that he was determined to march towards Salonika,

73

and would afterwards attend to his other affairs. Sire," said Boniface, Marquis of Montferrat, " I pray thee, since I am able without thee to get possession of my land, that thou wilt not enter therein; but if thou dost enter therein, I shall deem that thou art not acting for my good. And be it known to thee that I shall not go with thee, but depart from among you." And the Emperor Baldwin replied that, notwithstanding all this, he should most certainly go.

Alas! how ill-advised were they, both the one and the other, and how great was the sin of those who caused this quarrel! For if God had not taken pity upon them, now would they have lost all the conquests they had made, and Christendom been in danger of ruin. So by ill fortune was there division between the Emperor Baldwin of Constantinople and Boniface, Marquis of Montferrat,-and by illadvice. . The Emperor Baldwin rode towards Salonika, as he devised, with all his people, and with all his power. And Boniface, the Marquis of Montferrat, went back, and he took with him a great number of right worthy people. With him went James of Avesnes, William of Champlitte, Hugh of Colemi, Count Berthold of Katzenellenbogen, and the greater part of those who came from the Empire of Germany and held with the marquis. Thus did the marquis ride back till he came to a castle, very goodly, very strong, and very rich, which is called Demotica; and it was surrendered by a Greek of the city, and when the marquis had entered therein he garrisoned it. Then because of their knowledge of the empress (his wife), the Greeks began to turn towards him, and to surrender to his rule from all the country round about, within a day or two's journey.

The Emperor Baldwin rode straight on to Salonika, and came to a castle called Christopolis, one of the strongest in the world. And it surrendered, and those of the city did homage to him. Afterwards he came to another place called Blache, which was very strong and very rich, and this too surrendered, and the people did homage. Next he came to Cetros, a city strong and rich, and it also came to his rule and order, and did homage. Then he rode to Salonika, and encamped before the city, and was there for three days. And those within surrendered the city, which was one of the best and wealthiest in Christendom at that day, on condition that

74

he would maintain the uses and customs theretofore observed by the Greek emperor.

MESSAGE OF THE CRUSADERS TO BONIFACE - HE SUSPENDS THE SIEGE OF ADRIANOPLE

While the Emperor Baldwin was thus at Salonika, and the land surrendering to his good pleasure and commandment, the Marquis Boniface of Montferrat, with all his people and a great quantity of Greeks who held to his side, marched to Adrianople and besieged it, and pitched his tents and pavilions round about. Now Eustace of Saubruic was therein, with the people whom the emperor had left there, and they mounted the walls and towers and made ready to defend themselves.

Then took Eustace of Saubruic two messengers and sent them, riding night and day, to Constantinople. And they came to the Doge of Venice, and to Count Louis, and to those who had been left in the city by the Emperor Baldwin, and told them that Eustace of Saubruic would have them know that the emperor and the marquis were embroiled together, and that the marquis had seized Demotica, which was one of the strongest castles in Roumania, and one of the richest, and that he was besieging them in Adrianople. And when those in Constantinople heard this they were moved with anger, for they thought most surely that all their conquests would be lost.

Then assembled in the palace of Blachernae the Doge of Venice, and Count Louis of Blois and Chartres, and the other barons that were in Constantinople; and much were they distraught, and greatly were they angered, and fiercely did they complain of those who had put enmity between the emperor and the marquis. At the prayer of the Doge of Venice and of Count Louis, Geoffry of Villehardouin, the Marshal of Champagne, was enjoined to go to the siege of Adrianople, and appease the war, if he could, because he was well in favour with the marquis, and therefore they thought he would have more influence than any other. And he, because of their prayers, and of their great need, said he would go willingly; and he took with him Manasses of l'Isle, who was one of the good knights of the host, and one of the most honoured.

75

So they departed from Constantinople, and rode day by day till they came to Adrianople, where the siege was going on. And when the marquis heard thereof, he came out of the camp and went to meet them. With him came James of Avesnes, and William of Champlitte, and Hugh of Colemi, and Otho of la Roche, who were the chief counsellors of the marquis. And when he saw the envoys, he did them much honour and showed them much fair seeming.

Geoffry the Marshal, with whom he was on very good terms, spoke to him very sharply, reproaching him with the fashion in which he had taken the land of the emperor and besieged the emperor's people in Adrianople, and that without apprising those in Constantinople, who surely would have obtained such redress as was due if the emperor had done him any wrong. And the marquis disculpated himself much, and said it was because of the wrong the emperor had done him that he had acted in such sort.

So wrought Geoffry, the Marshal of Champagne, with the help of God, and of the barons who were in the confidence of the marquis, and who loved the said

Geoffry well, that the marquis assured him he would leave the matter in the hands of the Doge of Venice, and of Count Louis of Blois and Chartres, and of Conon of Béthune, and of Geoffry of Villehardouin, the Marshal-all of whom well knew what was the covenant made between himself and the emperor. So was a truce established between those in the camp and those in the city.

And you must know that Geoffry the Marshal, and Manasses of l'Isle, were right joyously looked upon, both by those in the camp and those in the city, for very strongly did either side wish for peace. And in such measure as the Franks rejoiced, so were the Greeks dolent, because right willingly would they have seen the Franks quarrelling and at war. Thus was the siege of Adrianople raised, and the marquis returned with all his people to Demotica, where was the empress his wife.

MESSAGE OF THE CRUSADERS TO BALDWIN - DEATH OF SEVERAL KNIGHTS

The envoys returned to Constantinople, and told what they had done. Greatly did the Doge of Venice, and Count Louis

76

of Blois, and all besides, then rejoice that to these envoys had been committed the negotiations for a peace; and they chose good messengers, and wrote a letter, and sent it to the Emperor Baldwin, tellin- him that the marquis had referred himself to them, with assurances that he would accept their arbitration, and that he (the emperor) was even more strongly bound to do the same, and that they besought him to do so-for they would in no wise countenance war-and promise to accept their arbitration, as the marquis had done.

While this was in progress the Emperor Baldwin had settled matters at Salonika and departed thence, garrisoning it with his people, and had left there as chief Renier of Mons, who was a good knight and a valiant. And tidings had come to him that the marquis had taken Demotica, and established himself therein, an(f conquered a great part of the land lying round about, and besieged the emperor's people in Adrianople. Greatly enraged was the Emperor Baldwin when these tidings came to him, and much did he hasten so as to raise the siege of Adrianople, and do to the marquis all the -harm that he could. Ah God! what mischief their discord might have caused! If God had not seen to it, Christendom would have been undone.

So did the Emperor Baldwin journey day by day. And a very great mischance had befallen those who were before Salonika, for many people of the host were stricken down with sickness. Many who could not be moved had to remain in the castles by which the emperor passed, and many were brought along in litters, journeying in sore pain; and many there were who died at Cetros (La Serre). Among those who so died at Cetros was Master ' John of Noyon, chancellor to the Emperor Baldwin. He was a good clerk, and very wise, and much had he comforted the host by the word of God, which he well knew how to preach. And you must know that by his death the good men of the host were much discomforted.

Nor was it long ere another great misfortune befell the host, for Peter of Amiens died, who was a man rich and noble, and a good and brave knight, and great dole was made for him by Hugh of St. Paul, who was his cousin-german; and heavily did his death weigh upon the host. Shortly after died Gerard of Mancicourt, who was a knight much

77

prized, and Giles of Annoy, and many other good people. Forty knights died during this expedition, and by their death was the host greatly enfeebled.

BALDWIN'S REPLY TO THE MESSAGE OF THE CRUSADERS

The Emperor Baldwin journeyed so day by day that he met the messengers sent by those of Constantinople. One of the messengers was a knight belonging to the land of Count Louis of Blois, and the count's liegeman; his name was Bègue of Fransures, and he was wise and eloquent. He spoke the message of his lord and the other barons right manfully, and said: " Sire, the Doge of Venice, and Count Louis, my lord, and the other barons who are in Constantinople send you health and greeting as to their lord, and they complain to God and to you of those who have raised discord between you and the Marquis of Montferrat, whereby it failed but little that Christendom was not undone; and they tell you that you did very ill when you listened to such counsellors. Now they apprise you that the marquis has referred to them the quarrel that there is between him and you, and they pray you, as their lord, to refer that quarrel to them likewise, and to promise to abide by their ruling. And be it known to you that they will in no wise, nor on any ground, suffer that you should go to war."

The Emperor Baldwin went to confer with his council, and said he would reply anon. Many there were in the emperor's council who had helped to cause the quarrel, and they were greatly outraged by the declaration sent by those at Constantinople, and they said: " Sire, you hear what they declare to you, that they will not suffer you to take vengeance of your enemy. Truly it seems that if you will not do as they order, they will set themselves against you."

Very many big words were then spoken; but, in the end, the council agreed that the emperor had no wish to lose the friendship of the Doge of Venice, and Count Louis, and the others who were in Constantinople; and the emperor replied to the envoys: " I will not promise to refer the quarrel to those who sent you, but I will go to Constantinople without doing aught to injure the marquis." So the Emperor Baldwin journeyed day by day till he came to Constantinople, and

78

the barons, and the other people, went to meet him, and received him as their lord with great honour.

RECONCILIATION OF BALDWIN AND BONIFACE

On the fourth day the emperor knew clearly that he had been ill-advised to quarrel with the marquis, and then the Doge of Venice and Count Louis came to speak to him and said: "Sire, we would pray you to refer this matter to us, as the marquis has done." And the emperor said he would do so right willingly. Then were envoys chosen to fetch the marquis, and bring him thither. Of them envoys one was Gervais of Chatel, and the second Renier of Trit, and Geoffry, Marshal of Champagne the third, and the Doge of Venice sent two of his people.

The envoys rode day by day till they came to Demotica, and they found the marquis with the empress his wife, and a great number of right worthy people, and they told him how they had come to fetch him. Then did Geoffry the Marshal desire him to come to Constantinople, as he had promised, and make peace in such wise as might be settled by those in whose hands he had remitted his cause; and they promised him safe conduct, as also to those who might go with him.

The marquis took counsel with his men. Some there were who agreed that he should go, and some who advised that he should not go. But the end of the debate was such that he went with the envoys to Constantinople, and took full a hundred knights with him; and they rode day by day till they came to Constantinople. Very gladly were they received in the city; and Count Louis of Blois and Chartres, and the Doge of Venice went out to meet the marquis, together with many other right worthy people, for he was much loved in the host.

Then was a parliament assembled, and the covenants were rehearsed between the Emperor Baldwin and the Marquis Boniface; and Salonika was restored to Boniface, with the land, he placing Demotica, which he had seized, in the hands of Geoffry the Marshal of Champagne, who undertook to keep it till he heard, by accredited messenger, or letters duly sealed, that the marquis was seized of Salonika, when he would give back Demotica to the emperor, or to whomsoever the emperor might appoint. Thus was peace made between the emperor and the marquis, as you have heard. And great was the joy

79

thereof throughout the host, for out of this quarrel might very great evil have arisen.

THE KINGDOM OF SALONIKA IS RESTORED TO BONIFACE - DIVISION OF THE LAND BETWEEN THE CRUSADERS

The marquis then took leave, and went towards Salonika with his people, and with his wife; and with him rode the envoys of the emperor; and as they went from castle to castle, each, with all its lordship, was restored to the marquis on the part of the emperor. So they came to Salonika, and those who held the place for the emperor surrendered it. Now the governor, whom the emperor had left there, and whose name was Renier of Mons, had died; he was a man most worthy, and his death a great mischance.

Then the land and country began to surrender to the marquis, and a great part thereof to come under his rule. But a Greek, a man of great rank, whose name was Leon Sgure, would in no wise come under the rule of the marquis, for he had seized Corinth and Napoli, two cities that lie upon the sea, and are among the strongest cities under heaven. He then refused to surrender, but began to make war against the marquis, and a very great many of the Greeks held with him. And another Greek, whose name was Michael, and who had come with the marquis from Constantinople, and was thought by the marquis to be his friend, he departed, without any word said, and went to a city called Arthe (? Durazzo) and took to wife the daughter of a rich Greek, who held the land from the emperor, and seized the land, and began to make war on the marquis.

Now the land from Constantinople to Salonika was quiet and at peace, for the ways were so safe that all could come and go at their pleasure, and from the one city to the other there were full twelve long days' journey. And so much time had now passed that we were at the beginning of September (1204). And the Emperor Baldwin was in Constantinople, and the land at peace, and under his rule. Then died two right good knights in Constantinople, Eustace of

Canteleu, and Aimery of Villeroi, whereof their friends had great sorrow.

Then did they begin to divide the land. The Venetians had their part,and the pilgrims the other. And when each

80

one was able to go to his own land, the covetousness of this world, which has worked so great evil, suffered them not to be at peace, for each began to deal wickedly in his land, some more, and some less, and the Greeks began to hate them and to nourish a bitter heart.

Then did the Emperor Baldwin bestow on Count Louis the duchy of Nice, which was one of the greatest lordships in the land of Roumania, and situate on the other side of the straits, towards Turkey. Now all the land on the other side of the straits had not surrendered to the emperor, but was against him. Then afterwards he gave the duchy of Philippopolis to Renier of Trit.

So Count Louis sent his men to conquer his land-some h.undred and twenty knights. And over them were set Peter of Bracieux and Payen of Orleans. They left Constantinople on All Saints Day (1st November 1204), and passed over the Straits of St. George on ship-board, and came to Piga, a city that lies on the sea, and is inhabited by Latins. And they began to war against the Greeks.

EXECUTION OF MOURZUPHLES AND IMPRISONMENT OF ALEXIUS

In those days it happened that the Emperor Mourzuphles, whose eyes had been put out-the same who had murdered his lord, the Emperor Isaac's son, the Emperor Alexius, whom the pilgrims had brought with them to that land-it happened, I say, that the Emperor Mourzuphles fled privily, and with but few people, and took refuge beyond the straits. But Thierri of Loos heard of it, for Mourzuphles' flight was revealed to him, and he took Mourzuphles and brought him to the Emperor Baldwin at Constantinople,. And the Emperor Baldwin rejoiced thereat, and took counsel with his men what he should do with a man who had been guilty of such a murder upon his lord.

And the council agreed to this: There was in Constantinople, towards the middle of the city, a column, one of the highest and the most finely wrought in marble that eye had ever seen; and Mourzuphles should be taken to the top of that column and made to leap down, in the sight of all the people, because it was fit that an act of justice so notable should be seen of the whole world. So they led the Emperor

Mourzuphles to the column, and took him to the top, and all the people in the city ran together to behold the event. Then they cast him down, and he fell from such a height that when he came to the earth he was all shattered and broken.

Now hear of a great marvel! On that column from which he fell were images of divers kinds, wrought in the marble. And among these images was one, worked in the shape of an emperor, falling headlong; for of a long time it had been prophesied that from that column an emperor of Constantinople should be cast down. So did the semblance and the prophecy come true.

It came to pass, at this time also, that the Marquis Boniface of Montferrat, who was near Salonika, took prisoner the Emperor Alexius-the same who had put out the eyes of the Emperor Isaac-and the empress his wife with him. And he sent the scarlet buskins, and the imperial vestments, to the Emperor Baldwin, his lord, at Constantinople, and the emperor took the act in very good part. Shortly after the marquis sent the Emperor Alexius and the empress his wife, to Montferrat, there to be imprisoned.

CAPTURE OF ABYDOS, OF PHILIPPOPOLIS, AND OF NICOMEDIA - THEODORE LASCARIS PRETENDS TO THE EMPIRE

At the feast of St. Martin after this (11th November 1204), Henry, the brother of the Emperor Baldwin, went forth from Constantinople, and marched down by the straits to the mouth of Abydos; and he took with him some hundred and twenty good knights. He crossed the straits near a city which is called Abydos, and found it well furnished with good things, with corn and meats, and with all things of which man has need. So he seized the city, and lodged therein, and then began to war with the Greeks who were before him. And the Armenians of the land, of whom there were many, began to turn towards him, for they greatly hated the Greeks.

At that time Renier of Trit left Constantinople, and went towards Philippopolis, which the emperor had given him; and he took with him some hundred and twenty very good knights, and rode day by day till he passed beyond Adrianople, and came to Philippopolis. And the people of the land received him, and obeyed him as their lord, for they beheld his coming very willingly. And they stood in great

need of succour, for Johannizza, the King of Wallachia, had mightily oppressed them with war. So Renier helped them right well, and held a great part of the land, and most of those who had sided with Johannizza, now turned to him. In those parts the war with Johannizza raged fiercely.

Tle emperor had sent some hundred knights over the straits of Saint George opposite Constantinople. Macaire of SainteMen,ehould was in command, and with him went Matthew of Wallincourt, and Robert of Ronsoi. They rode to a city called Nicomedia, which lies on a gulf of the sea, and is well two days' journey from Constantinople. When the Greeks saw them coming, they avoided the city, and went away; so the pilgrims lodged therein, and garrisoned it, and enclosed it with walls, and began to wage war before them, on that side also.

The land on the other side of the straits had for lord a Greek named Theodore Lascaris. He had for wife the daughter of the Emperor Alexius, through whom he laid claim to the land - this was the Alexius whom the Franks had driven from Constantinople, and who had put out his brother's eyes. The same Lascaris maintained the war against the Franks on the other side of the straits, in whatsoever part they might be.

In Constantinople remained the Emperor Baldwin and Count Louis, with but few people, and the Count of St. Paul, who was grievously sick with gout, that held him by the knees and feet; and the Doge of Venice, who saw naught.

REINFORCEMENTS FROM SYRIA - DEATH OF MARY, THE WIFE OF BALDWIN

After this time came from the land of Syria a great company of those who had abandoned the host, and gone thither from other ports than Venice. With this company came Stephen of Perche, and Renaud of Montmirail, who was cousin to Count Louis, and they were by him much honoured, for he was very glad of their coming. And the Emperor Baldwin, and the rest of the people also received them very gladly, for they were of high rank, and very rich, and brouaht very many good people with them.

From the land of Syria came Hugh of Tabarie, and Raoul his brother, and Thierri of Tenremonde, and very many people of the land, knights and light horsemen, and sergeants.

83

And the Emperor Baldwin gave to Stephen of Perche the duchy of Philadelphia.

Among other tidings came news at this time to the Emperor Baldwin whereby he was made very sorrowful; for the Countess Mary *[She was the daughter of Henry Count of Champagne and of Mary, daughter of Philip Augustus, King of France]* his wife, whom he had left in Flanders, seeIng she could not go with him because she was with childhe was then but count-had brought forth a daughter-and afterwards, on her recovery, she started to go to her lord overseass and passed to the port of Marseilles, and coming to Acre, she had but just landed, when the tidings came to her from Constantinople-told by the messengers whom her lord had sent-that Constantinople was taken, and her lord made emperor, to the great joy of all Christendom. On hearing this the lady was minded to come to him forthwith. Then a sickness took her, and she made an end and died, whereof there was great dole throughout all Christendom, for she was a gracious and virtuous lady and greatly honoured. And those who came in this company brought the tidings of her death, whereof the Emperor Baldwin had sore affliction, as also the barons of the land, for much did they desire to have her for their lady.

DEFEAT OF THEODORE AND CONSTANTINE LASCARIS

At that time those who had gone to the city of Piga - Peter of Bracieux and Payen of Orléans being the chiefs - fortified a castle called Palormo; and they left therein a garrison of their people, and rode forward to conquer the land. Theodore Lascaris had collected all the people he could, and on the day of the feast, of our Lord St. Nicholas (6th December 1204), which is before the Nativity, he joined battle in the plain before a castle called Poemaninon. The battle was engaged with great disadvantage to our people, for those of the other part were in such numbers as was marvellous; and on our side there were but one hundred and forty knights, without counting the mounted sergeants.

But our Lord orders battles as it pleases Him. By His grace and by His will, the Franks vanquished the Greeks and discomfited them, so that they suff ered very great loss. And within the week, they surrendered a very large part of the land. They surrendered Poemaninon, which was a very

84

strong castle, and Lopadium, which was one of the best cities of the land, and Polychna, which is seated on a lake of fresh water, and is one of the strongest and best castles that can be found. And you must know that our people fared very excellently, and by God's help had their will of that land.

Shortly after-, by the advice of the Armenians, Henry, the brother of the Emperor Baldwin of Constantinople, started from the city of Abydos, leaving therein a garrison of his people, and rode to a city called Adramittium, which lies on the sea, a two days' journey from Abydos. This city yielded to him, and he lodged therein, and a great part of the land surrendered; for the city was well supplied with corn and meats, and other goods. Then he maintained the war in those parts against the Greeks.

Theodore Lascaris, who had been discomfited at Poemaninon, collected as many people as he could, and assembled a very great army, and gave the command thereof to Constantine, his brother, who was one of the best Greeks in Roumania, and then rode straight towards Adramittium. And Henry, the brother of the Emperor Baldwin, had knowledge, through the Armenians, that a great host was marching against him, so he made ready to meet them, and set his battalions in order; and he had with him some very good men, as Baldwin of Beauvoir, and Nicholas of Mailly, and Anseau of Cayeux, and Thierri of Loos, and Thierri of Tenremonde.

So it happened that on the Saturday which is before mid Lent (19th March 1205), came Constantine Lascaris with his great host, before Adramittium. And Henry, when he knew of his coming, took counsel, and said he would not suff er himself to be shut up in the city, but would issue forth. And those of the other part came on with all their host, in great companies of horse and foot, and those on our part went out to meet them, and began the onslaught. Then was there a dour battle and fighting hand to hand; but by God's help the Franks prevailed, and discomfited their foes, so that many were killed and taken captive, and there was much booty. Then were the Franks at ease, and very rich, so that the people of the land turned to them, and began to bring in their rents.

85

BONIFACE ATTACKS LEON SGURE; HE IS JOINED BY GEOFFRY OF VILLEHARDOUIN, THE NEPHEW

Now let us leave speaking further (for the nonce), of those at Constantinople, and return to the Marquis Boniface of Montferrat. The marquis had gone, as you have heard, towards Salonika, and then ridden forth against Leon Sgure, who held Napoli and Corinth, two of the strongest cities in the world. Boniface besieged both cities at once. James of Avesnes, with many other good men, remained before Corinth, and the rest encamped before Napoli, and laid siege to it.

Then befell a certain adventure in the land. For Geoffry of Villehardouin, who was nephew to Geofiry of Villehardouin, Marshal of Roumania and Champagne, being his brother's son, was moved to leave Syria with the company that came to Constantinople. But wind and chance carried him to the port of Modon, and there his ship was injured, so that, of necessity, it behoved him to winter in that country. And a Greek, who was a great lord of the land, knew of it, and came to him, and did him much honour, and said: " Fair Sir, the Franks have conquered Constantinople, and elected an emperor. If thou wilt make alliance with me, I will deal with thee in all good faith, and we together Will conquer much land." So they made alliance on oath, the Greek and Geoffry of Villehardouin, and conquered together a great part of the country, and Geoffry of Villehardouin found much good faith in the Greek.

But adventures happen as God wills, and sickness laid hold of the Greek, and he made an end and died. And the Greek's son rebelled against Geoffry of ViHehardouin, and betrayed him, and the castles in which Geoffry had set a garrison turned against him. Now he heard tell that the marquis was besieging Napoli, so he went towards him with as many men as he could collect, and rode through the land for some six days in very great peril, and thus came to the carnp, where he was received right willingly, and much honoured by the marquis and all who were there. And this was but right, seeing he was very honourable and valiant, and a good knight.

86

EXPLOITS OF WILLIAM OF CHAMPLITTE AND GEOFFRY OF VILLEHARDOUIN, THE NEPHEW, IN MOREA

The marquis would have given him land and possessions so that he might remain with him, but he would not, and spoke to William of Champlitte, who was his friend, and said: " Sir, I come from a land that is very rich, and is called Morea. Take as many men as you can collect, and leave this host, and let us go and conquer that land by the help of God. And that which you will give me out of our conquests, I will hold from you, and I will be your liegeman." knd William of Champlitte, who greatly trusted and loved him, went to the marquis, and told him of the matter, and the marquis allowed of their going.

So William of Champlitte and Geoffry of Villehardouin (the nephew) departed from the host, and took with them about a hundred knights, and a great number of mounted sergeants, and entered into the land of Morea, and rode onwards till they came to the city of Modon. Michael heard that they were in the land with so few people, and he collected together a great number of people, a number that was marvellous, and he rode after them as one thinking they were all no better than prisoners, and in his hand.

And when they heard'tell that he was coming, they refortified Modon, where the defences had long since been pulled down, and there left their baggage, and the lesser folk. Then they rode out a day's march, and ordered their array with as many people as they had. But the odds seemed too great, for they had no more than five hundred men mounted, whereas on the other part there were well over five thousand. But events happen as God pleases; for our people fought with the Greeks ' and discomfited and conquered them. And the Greeks lost very heavily, while those on our side gained horses and arms enough, and other goods in very great plenty, and so returned very happy, and very joyously, to the city of Modon.

Afterwards they rode to a city called Coron, on the sea, and besieged it. And they had not besieged it long before it surrendered, and William gave it to Geoffry of Villehardouin (the nephew) and he became his liegeman, and set therein a garrison of his men. Next they went to a castle called Chale-

87

mate which was very strong and fair, and besieged it. This castle troubled them for a very long space, but they remained before it till it was taken. Then did more of the Greeks of that land surrender than had done aforetiine.

SIEGE OF NAPOLI AND CORINTH; ALLIANCE BETWEEN THE GREEKS AND JOHANNIZZA

The Marquis of Montferrat besieged Napoli, but he could there do nothing, for the place was too strong, and his men suffered greatly. James of Avesnes, meanwhile, continued to besiege Corinth, where he had been left by the marquis. Leon Sgure, who was in Corinth, and very wise and wily, saw that James had not many people with him, and did not keep good watch. So one morning, at the break of day, he issued from the city in force, and got as far as the tents, and killed many before they could get to their armour. . There was killed Dreux of Estruen, who was very honourable and valiant, and greatly was he lamented. And James of Avesnes, who was in command, waxed very wroth at the death of his knight, and did not leave the fray till he was wounded in the leg right grievously. And well did those who were present bear witness that it was to his doughtiness that they owed their safety; for you must know that they came very near to being all lost. But by God's help they drove the Greeks back into the castle by force.

Now the Greeks, who were very disloyal, still nourished treachery in their hearts. They perceived at that time that the Franks were so scattered over the land that each had his own matters to attend to. So they thought they could the more easily betray them. They took envoys therefore privily, from all the cities in the land, and sent them to Johannizza, the King of Wallachia and

79

Bulgaria, who was still at war with them as he had been aforetime. And they told Johannizza they would make him emperor, and give themselves wholly to him, and slay all the Franks. So they swore that they would obey him as their lord, and he swore that he would defend them as though they were his own people. Such was the oath sworn.

88

UPRISING OF THE GREEKS AT DEMOTICA AND ADRIANOPLE; THEIR DEFEAT AT ARCADIOPOLIS

At that time there happened a great misfortune at Constantinople, for Count Hugh of St. Paul, who had long been in bed, sick of the gout, made an end and died; and this caused great sorrow, and was a great mishap, and much was he bewept by his men and by his friends. He was buried with great honour in the church of our Lord St. George of Mangana.

Now Count Hugh in his lifetime had held a castle called Demotica, which was very strong and rich, and he had therein some of his knights and sergeants. The Greeks, who had made oath to the King of Wallachia that they would kill and betray the Franks, betrayed them in that castle, and slaughtered many and took many captive. Few escaped, and those who escaped went flying to a city called Adrianople, which the Venetians held at that time.

Not long after the Greeks in Adrianople rose in arms; and such of our men as were therein, and had been set to guard it, came out in great peril, and left the city. Tidings thereof came to the Emperor Baldwin of Constantinople, who had but few men with him, he and Count Louis of Blois. Much were they then troubled and dismayed. And thenceforth, from day to day, did evil tidings begin to come to them, that everywhere the Greeks were rising, and that wherever the Greeks found Franks occupying the land, they killedthem.

And those who had left Adrianople, the Venetians and the others who were there, came to a city called Tzurulum, that belonged to the Emperor Baldwin. There they found William of Blanvel, who kept the place for the emperor. By the help and comfort that he gave them, and because he accompanied them with as many men as he could, they turned back to a city, some twelve lea-ues distant, called Arcadiopolis, which belonged to the Venetians, and they found it empty. So they entered in, and put a garrison there.

On the third day the Greeks of the land gathered together, and came at the break of dawn before Arcadiopohs; and then began, from all sides, an assault, great and marvellous. The Franks defended themselves right well, and opened their

80

gates, and issued forth, attacking vigorously. As was God's will, the Greeks were discomfited, and those on our side began to cut them down and to slay them, and then chased them for a league, and killed many, and captured many horses and much other spoil.

So the Franks returned with great joy to Arcadiopolis, and sent tidings of their victory to the Emperor Baldwin, in Constantinople, who was much rejoiced tliereat. Nevertheless they dared not hold the city of Arcadiopolis, but left it on the morrow, and abandoned it, and returned to the city of Tzurulum. Here they remained in very great doubt, for they misdoubted the Greeks who were in the city as much as those who were without, because the Greeks in the city had also taken part in the oath sworn to the King of Wallachia, and were bound to betray the Franks. And manv there were who did not dare to abide in Tzurulum, but made their way back to Constantinople.

THE CRUSADERS ON THE OTHER SIDE OF THE STRAITS ARE RECALLED TO MARCH ON ADRIANOPLE - EXPEDITION OF GEOFFRY OF VILLEHARDOUIN

Then the Emperor Baldwin and the Doge of Venice, and Count Louis took counsel together, for they saw they were losing the whole land. And they settled that the emperor should tell his brother Henry, who was at Adramittium, to abandon whatsoever conquests he had made, and come to their succour.

Count Louis, on his side, sent to Payen of Orléans and Peter of Bracieux, who were at Lopadium, and to all the people that were with them, telling them to leave whatsoever conquests they had made, save Pioa only, that lay on the sea, where they were to set a garrison - the smallest they could - and that the remainder were to come to their succour.

The emperor directed Macaire of Sainte-Menchould, and Matthew of Wallincourt, and Robert of Ronsoi, who had some hundred knights with them in Nicomedia, to leave Nicomedia and come to their succour.

By command of the Emperor Baldwin, Geoffry of Villehardouin, Marshal of Champagne and of Roumania, issued from Constantinople, with Manasses of l'Isle, and Nvith as many men as they could corect, and these were few enough, seeing

that all the land was being lost. And they rode to the city of Tzurulum, which is distant a three days' journey. There they found William of Blanvel, and those that were with him, in very great fear, and much were these reassured at their coming. At that place they remained four days. The Emperor Baldwin sent after Geoffry the Marshal as many as he could, of such people as were coming into Constantinople, so that on the fourth day there were at Tzurulum eighty knights.

Then did Geoffry the Marshal move forward, and Manasses of l'Isle, and their people, and they rode on, and came to the city of Arcadiopolis, and quartered themselves therein. There they remained a day, and then moved to a city called Bulgaropolis. The Greeks had avoided this city and the Franks quartered themselves therein. The following day they rode to a city called Neguise, which was very fair and strong, and well furnished with all good things. And they found that the Greeks had abandoned it, and were all gone to Adrianople. Now Adrianople was distant nine French leagues, and therein were gathered all the great multitude of the Greeks. And the Franks decided that they should wait where they were till the coming of the Emperor Baldwin.

RENIER OF TRIT ABANDONED AT PHILIPPOPOLIS BY HIS SON AND THE GREATER PART OF HIS PEOPLE

Now does this book relate a great marvel: for Renier of Trit, who was at Philippopolis, a good nine days' journey from Constantinople, with at least one hundred and twenty knights, was deserted by Reginald his son, and Giles his brother, and James of Bondies, who was his nephew, and Achard of Verdun, who had his daughter to wife. And they had taken some thirty of his knights, and thought to come to Constantinople; and they had left him, you must know, in great peril. But they found the country raised against them, and were discomfited; and the Greeks took them, and afterwards handed them over to the King of Wallachia, who had their heads cut off. And you must know that they were but little pitied by the people, because they had behaved in such evil sort to one whom they were bound to treat quite otherwise.

And when the other knights of Renier de Trit saw that he

91

was thus abandoned by those who were much more bound to him than themselves, they felt the less shame, and some eighty together left him, and departed by another way. So Renier of Trit remained among the Greeks with very few men, for he had not more than fifteen knights at Philippopolis and Stanimac-which is a very strong castle which he held, and where he was for a long time besieged.

BALDWIN UNDERTAKES THE SIEGE OF ADRIANOPLE

We will speak no further now of Renier of Trit but return to the Emperor Baldwin, who is in Constantinople, with but very few people, and greatly angered and much distracted. He was waiting for Henry his brother, and all the people on the other side of the straits, and the first who came to him from the other side of the straits came from Nicomedia, viz.: Macaire of Sainte-Menehould, and Matthew of Wallincourt, and Robert of Ronsoi, and with them full a hundred knights.

When the emperor saw them, he was right glad, and he consulted with Count Louis, who was Count of Blois and Chartres. And they settled to go forth, with as many men as they had, to follow Geoffry the Marshal of Champagne, who had gone before. Alas 1 what a pity it was they did not wait till all had joined them who were on the other side of the straits, seeing how few people they had, and how perilous the adventure on which they were bound.

So they started from Constantinople, some one hundred and forty knights, and rode from day to day till they came to the castle of Neguise, where Geoffry the Marshal was quartered. That night they took counsel together, and the decision to which they came was, that on the morrow they should go before Adrianople, and lay siege to it. So they ordered their battalions, and did for the best with such people as they had.

When the morning came, and full daylight, they rode as had been arranged, and came before Adrianople. And they found it very well defended, and saw the flags of Johannizza, King of Wallachia and Bulgaria, on the walls and towers; and the city was very strong and very rich, and very full of people. Then they made an assault, with very few people, before two of the gates, and this was on the Tuesday of

92

Palmtide (29th March I205). So did they remain before the city for three days, in great discomfort, and but few in number.

THE SIEGE OF ADRIANOPLE CONTINUED WITHOUT RESULT

Then came Henry Dandolo, the Doge of Venice, who was' an old man and saw naught. And he brought with him as many people as he had, and these were quite as many as the Emperor Baldwin and Count Louis had brought, and he encamped before one of the gates. On the morrow they were joined by a troop of mounted sergeants, but these might well have been better men than they proved themselves to be. And the host *[note: meaning here a little obscure. I think, however, the intention of the origin'd is to state that the host, and not only the sergeants, lacked supplies]* had small store of provisions, because the merchants could not come with them; nor could they go foraginc, because of the many Greeks that were spread throughout the land.

Johannizza, King of Wallachia, was coming to succour Adrianople with a very great host; for he brought with him Wallachians and Bulgarians, and full fourteen thousand Comans who had never been baptised.

Now because of the dearth of provisions, Count Louis of Blois and Chartres went foraging on Palm Sunday. With him went Stephen of Perche, brother of Count Geoffry of Perche, and Renaud of Montmirail, who was brother of Count Hervée of Nevers, and Gervais of Châtel, and more than half of the host. They went to a castle called Peutace, and found it well garrisoned with Greeks, and assailed it with great force and fury; but they were able to achieve nothing, and so retreated without taking anv spoils. Thus they remained during the week of the two'Easters (Palm Sunday to Easter Day), and fashioned engines of divers sorts, and set such miners as they had to work underground and so undermine the wall. And thus did they celebrate Easter (10th April) before Adrianople, being but few in number and scant of provisions.

93

JOHANNIZZA, KING OF WALLACHIA, COMES TO RELIEVE ADRIANOPLE

Then came tidings that Johannizza, King of Wallachia, was coming upon them to relieve the city. So they set their affairs in order, and it was arranged that Geoffry the Marshal, and Manasses of l'Isle should guard the camp, and that the Emperor Baldwin and all the remainder of the host should issue from the camp if so be that johanizza came and offered battle.

Thus they remained till the Wednesday of Easter week, and Johannizza had by that time approached so near that he encamped at about five leagues from us. And he sent his Comans running before our camp, and a cry was raised throughout the camp, and our men issued therefrom helterskelter, and pursued the Comans for a full league very foolishly; for when they wished to return, the Comans began to shoot at them in grievous wise, and wounded a good many of their horses.

So our men returned to the camp, and the barons were summoned to the quarters of the Emperor Baldwin. And they took counsel, and all said that they had dealt foolishly in thus pursuing people who were so lightly armed. And in the end they settled that if Johannizza came on again, they would issue forth, and set themselves in array of battle before the camp, and there wait for him, and not move from thence. And they had it proclaimed throughout the host that none should be so rash as to disregard this order, and move from his post for any cry or tumult that might come to his ears. And it was settled that Geoffry the Marshal should keep guard on the side of the city, with Manasses of l'Isle.

So they passed that night till the Thursday morning in Easter week, when they heard mass and ate their dinner. And the Comans ran up to their tents, and a cry arose, and they ran to arms, and issued from the camp with all their battalions in array, as had afore been devised.

94

DEFEAT OF THE CRUSADERS-BALDWIN TAKEN PRISONER

Count Louis went out first with his battalion, and began to follow after the Comans, and sent to urge the emperor to come after him. Alas! how ill did they keep to what had been settled the night before! For they ran in pursuit of the Comans for at least two leagues, and joined issue with them, and chased them a long space. And then the Comans turned back upon them, and began to cry out and to shoot.

On our side there were battalions made up of other people than knights, people having too little knowledge of arms, and they began to wax afraid and be discomfited. And Count Louis, who had been the first to attack, was wounded in two places full sorely; and the Comans and Wallachians began to invade our ranks; and the count had fallen, and one of his knights, whose name was John of Friaise, dismounted, and set him on his horse. Many were Count Louis' people who said: "Sir, get you hence, for you are too sorely wounded, and in two places." And he said: "The Lord God forbid that ever I should be reproached with flying from the field, and abandoning the emperor."

The emperor, who was in great straits on his side, recalled his people, and he told them that he would not fly, and that they were to remain with him: and well do those who were there present bear witness that never did knight defend himself better with his hands than did the emperor. This combat lasted a long time. Some were there who did well, and some were there who fled. In the end, for so God suffers misadventures to occur, they were discomfited. There on the field remained the Emperor Baldwin, who never would fly, and Count Louis; the Emperor Baldwin was taken alive and Count Louis was slain.

Alas! how woful was our loss! There was lost the Bishop Peter of Bethlehem, and Stephen of Perche, brother to Count Geoffry, and Renaud of Montmirail, brother of the Count of Nevers, and Matthew of Wallincourt, and Robert of Ronsoi, John of Friaise, Walter of Neuilli, Ferri of Yerres, John his brother, Eustace of Heumont, John his brother, Baldwin of Neuville, and many more of whom the book does

95

not here make mention. Those who were able to escape, they came back flying to the camp.

THE CRUSADERS RAISE THE SIEGE OF ADRIANOPLE

When Geoffry the Marshal of Champagne, who was keeping guard at one of the gates of the cityo , saw this he issued from the camp as soon as he could, with all the men that were with him, and gave command to Manasses of lisle, who was on guard at another gate, that he should follow after him. And he rode forth with all his force at full speed, and in full array, to meet the fugitives, and the fugitives all rallied round him. And Manasses of l'Isle followed as soon as he was able, with his men, and joined himself to him, so that together they formed a very strong body; and all those who came out of the rout, and whom they could stop, were taken into their ranks.

The rout was thus stayed between Nones and Vespers. But the most part of the fugitives were so afeared that they fled right before them till they came to the tents and quarters. Thus was the rout stayed, as you have heard; and the Comans, with the Wallachians and Greeks, who were in full chace, ceased their pursuit. But these still galled our force with their bows and arrows, and the men of our force kept still with their faces turned towards them. Thus did both sides remain till nightfall, when the Comans and Wallachians began to retire.

Then did Geoffry of Villehardouin, the Marshal of Champagne and Roumania, summon to the camp the Doge of Venice, who was an old man and saw naught, but very wise and brave and vigorous; and he asked the Doge to come to him there where he stood with his men, holding the field; and the Doge did so. And when the Marshal saw him, he called him into council, aside, all alone, and said to him: "Lord, you see the misadventure that has befallen us. We have lost the Emperor Baldwin and Count Louis, and the larger part of our people, and of the best. Now let us bethink ourselves how to save what is left. For if God does not take pity of them, we are but lost."

And in the end they settled it thus: that the Dogė would return to the camp, and put heart into the people, and order that every one should arm and remain quiet in his tent or

96

pavilion; and that Geoffry the Marshal would remain in full order of battle before the camp till it was night, so that their enemies might not see the host move; and that when it was night all would move from before the city; the Doge of Venice would go before, and Geoffry the Marshal would form the rear-guard, with those who were with him.

RETREAT OF THE CRUSADERS

Thus they waited till it was night; and when it was night the Doge of Venice left the camp, as had been arranged, and Geoffry the Marshal formed the rear-guard. And they departed at foot pace, and took with them all their people mounted and dismounted, the wounded as well those who were whole-they left not one behind. And they journeyed towards a city that lies upon the sea, called Rodosto, and that was full three days' journey distant. So they departed from Adrianople, as you have heard; and this adventure befell in the year of the Incarnation of Jesus Christ twelve hundred and five.

And in the night that the host left Adrianople, it happened that a company started to get to Constantinople earlier, and by a more direct way; and they were greatly blamed therefor. In this company was a certain count from Lombardy named Gerard, who came from the land of the marquis, and Odo of Ham, who was lord of a castle called Ham in Vermandois, and John of Maseroles, and many others to the number of twenty-five knights, whom the book does not name. And they went away so fast after the discomfiture, which had taken place on the Thursday evening, that they came to Constantinople on the Saturday night, though it was ordinarilyagoodfivedays'journey. Andtheytoldthenews to the Cardinal Peter of Capua, who was there by the authority of Innocent Pope of Rome, and to Conon of Béthune, who guarded the city, and to Miles the Brabant, and to the other good men in the city. And you must know that these were greatly affeared, and thought of a certainty that all the rest, who had been left before Adrianople, were lost, for they had no news of them.

97

PETER OF BRACIEUX AND PAYEN OF ORLEANS MEET THE RETREATING HOST

Now will we say no more about those at Constantinople, who were in sore trouble, but go back to the Doge of Venice and Geoffry the Marshal, who marched all the night that they left Adrianople, till the dawn of the following day; and then they came to a city called Pamphyle. Now listen and you shall hear how adventures befall as God wills: for in that city had lain during the night, Peter of Bracieux and Payen of Orldans, and all the men belonging to the land of Count Louis, at least a hundred very good knights and one hundred and forty mounted sergeants, and they were coming from the other side of the straits to join the host at Adrianople.

When they saw the host coming, they ran to their arms nght nimbly, for they thought we were the Greeks. So they armed themselves, and sent to know what people we were, when their messengers discovered that we were the host retreating after our discomfiture. So the messengers went back, and told them that the Emperor Baldwin was lost, and their lord Count Louis, of whose land and country they were, and of whose following.

Sadder news could they not have heard. There might you have seen many tears wept, and many hands wrung for sorrow and pity. And they went on, all an-ned as they were, till they came to where Geoffry, the Marshal of Champagne, was keeping guard in the rear, in very great anxiety and misease. For Johannizza, the King of Wallachia and Bulgaria, had come at the point of day before Adrianople with all his host, and found that we had departed, and so ridden after us till it was full day; and when he found us not, he was full of grief; and well was it that he found us not, for if he had found us we must all have been lost beyond recovery.

"Sir," said Peter of Bracieux and Payen of Orléans to Geoffry the Marshal, "what would you have us do? We will do whatever you wish." And he answered them: " You see how matters stand with us. You are fresh and unwearied, and your horses also; therefore do you keep guard in the rear, and I will go forward and hold in hand our people, who are greatly dismayed and in sore need of comfort." To this they consented right willingly. So they

98

established the rearguard duly and efficiently, and as men who well knew how, for they were good knights and honourable.

THE HOST REACHES RODOSTO

Geoffry the Marshal rode before and led the host, and rode till he came to a city called Cariopolis. Then he saw that the horses were weary with marching all night, and entered into the city, and put them up till noon. And they gave food to their horses, and ate themselves of what they could find, and that was but little.

So they remained all the day in that city until night. And Johannizza, the King of Wallachia, had followed them all the day with all his powers, and encamped about two leaaues from them. And when it was night, those in the city all armed themselves and departed. Geoffry the Marshal led the van, and those formed the rear-guard who had formed it during the day. So they rode through that night, and the following day (16th April) in great fear and much hardship, till they came to the city of Rodosto, a city very rich and very strong, and inhabited by Greeks. These Greeks did not dare to defend themselves, so our people entered in and took quarters; so at last were they in safety.

Thus did the host escape from Adrianople, as you have heard. Then was a council held in the city of Rodosto; and it seemed to the council that Constantinople was in greater jeopardy than they were. So they took messengers, and sent them by sea, telling them to travel night and day, and to advise those in the city not to be anxious about them-for they had escaped-and that they would repair back to Constantinople as soon as they could.

SEVEN THOUSAND PILGRIMS LEAVE THE CRUSADERS

At the time when the messengers arrived, there were in Constantinople five ships of Venice, very large and very good, laden with pilgrims, and knights and sergeants, who were leaving the land and returning to their own countries. There were at least seven thousand men at arms in the ships, and one was William the advocate of Béthune, and there were besides Baldwin of Aubigny, and John of Virsin, who be-

99

longed to the land of Count Louis, and was his liegeman, and at least one hundred other knights, whom the book does not here name. Master Peter of Capua, who was cardinal from the Pope of Rome, Innocent, and Conon of Béthune, who commanded in Constantinople, and Miles the Brabant, and a great number of other men of mark, went to the five ships, and prayed those who were in them, with sighs and tears, to have mercy and pity upon Christendom, and upon their liege lords who had been lost in battle, and to remain for the love of God. But they would not listen to a single word, and left the port. They spread their sails, and went their way, as God ordained, in such sort that the wind took them to the port of Rodosto; and this was on the day following that on which those who had escaped from the discomfiture came thither.

The same prayers, with tears and weeping, that had been addressed to them at Constantinople-those same prayers were now addressed to them at Rodosto; and Geoffry the Marshal, and those who were with him, besought them to have mercy and pity on the land, and remain, for never would they be able to succour any land in such dire need. They replied that they would consult together, and give an answer on the morrow.

And now listen to the adventure which befell that night in the city. There was a knight from the land of Count Louis, called Peter of Frouville, who was held in honour, and of great name. The same fled by night, and left all his baggage and his people, and gat himself to the ship of John of Virsin, who was from the land of Count Louis of Blois and Chartres. And those on board the five ships, who in the morning were to give their answer to Geoffry the Marshal and to the Doge of Venice, so soon as they saw the day, they spread their sails, and went their way without word said to any one. Much and great blame did they receive, both in the land whither they went, and in the land they had left; and he who received most blame of all was Peter of Frouville. For well has it been said that he is but ill-advised who, through fear of death, does what will be a reproach to him for ever.

100

MEETING OF MANY OF THE CRUSADERS-HENRY, THE BROTHER OF BALDWIN, IS MADE REGENT

Now let us speak of these last no farther, but speak of Henry, brother to the Emperor Baldwin of Constantinople, who had left Adramittium, which he had conquered, and passed the straits at the city of Abydos, and was coming towards Adrianople to succour the Emperor Baldwin, his brother. And with him had come the Armenians of the land, who had helped him against the Greeks-some twenty thousand with all their wives and children-for they dared not remain behind.

Then came to him the news, by certain Greeks, who had escaped from the discomfiture, that his brother the Emperor Baldwin was lost, and Count Louis, and the other barons. Afterwards came the news of those who had escaped and were at Rodosto; and these asked him to make all the haste he could, and come to them. And because he wanted to hasten as much as he could, and reach them earlier, he left behind the Armenians, who travelled on foot, and had with them chariots, and their wives and children; and inasmuch as these could not come on so fast, and he thought they would travel safely and without hurt, he went forward and encamped in a village called Cartopolis.

On that very day came thither the nephew of Geoffry the Marshal, Anseau of Courcelles, whom Geoffry had summoned from the parts of Macre, Trajanopolis, and the Baie, lands that had been bestowed upon him; and with Anseau came the people from PhilippoPolis, who had left Renier of Trit. This company held full a hundred good knights, and full five hundred mounted sergeants, who all were on their way to Adrianople to succour the Emperor Baldwin. But tidings had come to them, as to the others, that the emperor had been defeated, so they turned to go to Rodosto, and came to encamp at Cartopolis, the village where Henry, the brother of the Emperor Baldwin, was then encamped. And when Baldwin's men saw them coming, they ran to arms, for they thought they were Greeks, and the others thought the same of Baldwin's men. And so they advanced till they became known to one another, and each was right glad of the other's coming, and felt all the safer; and they quartered themselves in the village that night until the morrow.

On the morrow they left, and rode straight towards Rodosto, and came that night to the city; and there they found the Doge of Venice and Geoffry the Marshal, and all who had escaped from the late discomfiture; and right glad were these to see them. Then were many tears shed for sorrow by those who had lost their friends. Ah, God! what pity it was that those men now assembled had not been at Adrianople with the Emperor Baldwin, for in that case would nothing have been lost. But such was not God's pleasure.

So they sojoumed there on the following day, and the day after, and arranged matters; and Henry, the brother of the Emperor Baldwin, was received into lordship, as regent of the empire, in lieu of his brother.

And then misfortune came upon the Armenians, who were coming after Henry, the brother of the Emperor Baldwin, for the people of the land gathered together and discomfited the Armenians, so that they were all taken, killed or lost.

RETURN TO CONSTANTINOPLE - APPEALS FOR HELP SENT TO THE POPE, AND TO FRANCE AND TO OTHER LANDS - DEATH OF THE DOGE

Johannizza., King of Wallachia and Bulgaria, had with him all his power, and he occupied the whole land; and the country, and the cities, and the castles held for him; and his Comans over-ran the land as far as Constantinople. Henry the regent of the empire, and the Doge of Venice, and Geoffry the Marshal, were still at Rodosto, which is a three days' journey from Constantinople. And they took council, and the Doge of Venice set a garrison of Venetians in Rodosto -for it was theirs. And on the morrow they put their forces in array, and rode, day by day, towards Constantinople.

When they reached Selymbria, a city which is two days' journey from Constantinople, and belonged to the Emperor Baldwin, Henry his brother set there a garrison of his people, and they rode with the rest to Constantinople, where they were received right willingly, for the people were in great terror. Nor is that to be wondered at, for they had lost so much of the country, that outside Constantinople they only held Rodosto and Selymbria; the whole of the rest of the country being held by Johannizza, King of Wallachia and Bulgaria. And on the other side of the straits of St. George, they held no more than the castle of Piga, while the rest of the land was in the hands of Theodore Lascaris.

Then the barons decided to send to the Apostle of Rome, Innocent, and to France and Flanders, and to other lands, to ask for succour. And for this purpose were chosen as envoys Nevelon, Bishop of Soissons, and Nicholas of Mailly, and John Bliaud. The rest remained in Constantinople, in great distress, as men who stood in fear of losing the land. So they remained till Pentecost (29th May 1205). And within this time a very great misfortune happened to the host, for Henry Dandolo was taken sick; so he made an end and died, and was buried with great honour in the church of St. Sophia.

When Pentecost had come, Johannizza, the King of Wallachia and Bulgaria, had pretty well had his will of the land; and he could no longer hold his Comans to-ether, because they were unable to keep the field during the summer; so the Comans departed to their own country. And he, with all his host of Bulgarians and Greeks, marched against the marquis towards Salonika. And the marquis, who had heard the news of the discomfiture of the Emperor Baldwin, raised the siege of Napoli, and went to Salonika with as many men as he could collect, and garrisoned it.

THE REGENT OBTAINS CERTAIN ADVANTAGES OVER THE GREEKS

Henry, the brother of the Emperor Baldwin of Constantinople, with as many people as he could gather, marched against the Greeks to a city called Tzurulum, which is a three days' journey from Constantinople. This city surrendered, and the Greeks swore fealty to him-an oath which at that time men observed badly. From thence he marched to Arcadiopolis, and found it void, for the Greeks did not dare to await his coming. And from thence again he rode to the city of Bizye, which was very strong, and well garrisoned with Greeks; and this city too surrendered. Aferwards he rode to the city of Napoli (Apros) which also remained well garrisoned with Greeks.

As our people were preparing for an assault, the Greeks within the city asked to negotiate for capitulation. But

103

while they thus negotiated, the men of the host effected an entrance into the city on another side, and Henry the Regent of the empire and those who were negotiating knew nothing of it. And this proved very disastrous to the Greeks. For the Franks, who had effected an entrance, began to slaughter them, and to seize their goods, and to take all that they had. So were many killed and taken captive. In this wise was Napoli (Apros) captured; and the host remained there three days. And the Greeks were so terrified by this slaughter, that they abandoned all the cities and castles of the land, and fled for refuge to Adrianople and Demotica, which were very strong and good cities.

SERES SURRENDERS TO JOHANNIZZA - HE FORFEITS HIS WORD

At that time it happened that Johannizza, the King of Wallachia and Bulgaria, with all his host, marched against the marquis, towards a city called Seres. And the marquis had set a strong garrison of his people in the city, for he had set there Hugh of Colemi, who was a very good knight, and hi,h in rank, and William of Arles, who was his marshal, and great part of his best men. And Johannizza, the King of Wallachia besieged them; nor had he been there long before he took the burgh by force. And at the taking of the burgh a great misfortune befell, for Hugh of Colemi was killed; he was struck through the eye.

When he was killed, who was the best of them all, the rest of the garrison were greatly afeared. They drew back into the castle, which was very strong; and Johannizza besieged them, and erected his petraries and mangonels. Nor had he besieged them long before they began to talk about surrendering, for which they were afterwards blamed, and incurred great reproach. And they agreed to yield up the castle to Johannizza, and Johannizza on his side caused twenty-five of the men of highest rank that he had to swear to them that they should be taken, safe and sound, with all their horses, and all their arms, and all their baggage, to Salonika, or Constantinople, or Hungary-wMchever of the three it liked them best.

In this manner was Seres surrendered, and Johannizza caused the besieged to come forth from the castle and en-

104

camp near him in the fields; and he treated them with much fair seeming, and sent them presents. So he kept them for three days, and then he lied and foreswore his promises; for he had them taken, and spoiled of their goods, and led away to Wallachia, naked, and unshod, and on foot. The poor and the mean people, who were of little worth, he sent into Hungary; and as for the others, he caused their heads to be cut off. Of such mortal treachery was the KinL, of Wallachia guilty, as you have heard. Here' did the host suffer grievous loss, one of the most dolorous that ever it suffered. And Johannizza had the castle and city razed, and went on after the marquis.

THE REGENT BESIEGES ADRIANOPLE IN VAIN

Henry, the Regent of the empire, with all his power, rode towards Adrianople, and laid siege to it; and he was in great peril, for there were many, both within and without the city who so hemmed him in, he and his people, that they could scantl buy provisions, or go foraging. Therefore they enclosed their camp with palisades and barriers, and told off part of their men to keep guard within the palisades and barriers, while the others attacked the city.

And they devised machines of divers kinds, and scaling ladders, and many other engines, and wrought diligently to take the city. But they could not take it, for the city was very strong and well furnished for defence. So matters went ill with them, and many of their people were wounded; and one of their good knights, Peter of Bracieux, was struck on the forehead from a mangonel, and brought near to death; but he recovered, by the will of God, and was taken away in a litter.

When they saw that they could in no wise prevail against the city, Henry the Regent of the empire, and the French host departed. And greatly were they harassed by the people of the land and by the Greeks; and they rode -from day to day till they came to a city called Pamphyle, and lodged there, and sojourned in it for two months. And they made thence many forays towards Demotica and the country round about, where they captured much cattle, and other booty. So the host remained in those parts till the beginning of winter; and supplies came to them from Rodosto, and from the sea.

105

DESTRUCTION OF PHILIPPOPOLIS BY JOHANNIZZA

Now let us leave speaking of Henry, the Regent of the empire, and speak of Johannizza, the King of Wallachia and Bulgaria, who had taken Seres, as you have already heard, and killed by treachery those who had surrendered to him. Afterwards he had ridden towards Salonika, and sojourned thereby a long while, and wasted a great part of tfle land. The Marquis Boniface of Montferrat was at Salonika, very wroth, and sorrowing greatly for the loss of his lord the Emperor Baldwin, and for the other barons, and for his castle of Seres that he had lost, and for his men.

And when Johannizza saw that he could do nothing more, he retired towards his own land, with all his force. And the people in Philippopolis-which belonged to Renier of Trit, for the Emperor Baldwin had bestowed it upon him-heard tell how the Emperor Baldwin was lost, and many of his barons, and that the marquis had lost Seres; and they saw that the relatives of Renier of Trit, and his own son and his nephew, had abandoned him, and that he had with him but very few people; and they deemed that the Franks would never be in power again. So a great part of the people, who were Paulicians, *[Note: An Eastern sect. They believed, among other things, that all matter is evil, and that Christ suffered in appearance only.]* betook themselves to Johannizza, and surrendered themselves to him, and said: " Sire, ride to Philippopolis, or send thither thy host, and we will deliver the whole city into thy hands."

When Renier of Trit, who was in the city, knew of this, he doubted not that they would yield up the city to Johannizza. So he issued forth with as many people as he could collect, and left at the point of day, and came to one of the outlying quarters of the city where dwelt the Paulicians who had repaired to Johannizza, and he set fire to that quarter of the city, and burned a great part of it. Then he went to the castle of Stanimac, which was at three leagues' distance, and garrisoned by his people, and entered therein. And in this castle he lay besieged for a long while, some thirteen months, in great distress and great poverty, so that for famine they ate their horses. He was distant a nine

106

days' journey from Constantinople, and could neither obtain tidings therefrom, nor send tidings thither.

Then did Johannizza send his host before Philippopolis; nor had he been there long before those who were in the city surrendered it to him, and he promised to spare their lives. And after he had promised to spare their lives, he first caused the archbishop of the city to be slain, and the men of rank to be flayed alive, and certain others to be burned, and certain others to have their heads cut off, and the rest he caused to be driven away in chains. And the city he caused to be pulled down, with its towers and walls; and the high palaces and rich houses to be burned and utterly destroyed. Thus was destroyed the noble city of Philippopolis, one of the three finest cities in the empire of Constantinople.

THE REGENT SETS GARRISONS IN SUCH PLACES AS HE STILL HELD

Now let us leave off speaking of those who were at Philippopolis, and of Renier of Trit, who is shut up in Stanimac, and return to Henry, the brother of the Emperor Baldwin, who had sojourned at Pamphyle till the beginning of winter. Then he took council with his men and with his barons; and they decided to set a garrison in a city called Rusium, which was situate at a place rich and fertile in the middle of the land; and the chiefs placed over this garrison were Thierri of Loos, who was seneschal, and Thierri of

Tenremonde, who was constable. And Henry,,the Regent of the empire, gave to them at least seven score knights, and a great many mounted sergeants, and ordered them to maintain the war against the Greeks, and to guard the marches.

And he himself went with the rest of his people to the city of Bizye, and placed a garrison there; and left in command Anseau of Cayeux, and confided to him at least six score knights, and a great many mounted sergeants. Another city, called Arcadiopolis was garrisoned by the Venetians. And the city of Napoli was restored by the brother of the Emperor Baldwin to Vernas, who had to wife the sister *[Agnes, sister to Philip Augustus, King of France]* of the King of France, and was a Greek who sided with us; and except he, no other Greek was on our part. And those who were in these cities maintained the war against the Greeks,

107

and made many forays. Henry himself returned to Constantinople with the rest of his men.

Now Johannizza, the King of Wallachia and Bulgaria, though rich and of great possessions, never forgat his own interests, but raised a great force of Comans and Wallachians. And when it came to three weeks after Christmas, he sent these men into the land of Roumania to help those at Adrianople and Demotica; and the latter, being now in force, grew bolder and rode abroad with the greater assurance.

DEFEAT OF THE FRANKS NEAR RUSIUM

Thierri of Tenremonde, who was chief and constable, made a foray on the fourth day before the feast of St. Mary Candlemas (30th January 1206); and he rode all night, having six score knights with him, and left Rusium with but a small garrison. When it was dawn, he came to a village where the Comans and Wallachians were encamped, and surprised them in such sort that those who were in the village were unaware of their coming. They killed a good many of the Comans and Wallachians, and captured some forty of their horses; and when they had done this execution, they turned back towards Rusium.

And on that very night the Comans and Wallachians had ridden forth to do us hurt; and there were some seven thousand of them. They came in the morning before Rusium, and were there a lono, space; and the garrison, which was but small, closed the gates, and mounted the walls; and the Comans and Wallachians turned back. They had not gone more than a league and a half from the city, when they met the company of the French under the command of Thierri of Tenremonde. So soon as the French saw them advancing, they formed into their four battalions, with intent to draw into Rusium in slow time; for they knew that if, by God's grace, they could come thither, they would then be in safety.

The Comans, and the Wallachians, and the Greeks of the land rode towards them, for they were in very great force. And they came upon the rear-guard, and began to harass it full sorely. Now the rear-guard was formed of the men of Thierri of Loos, who was seneschal, and had returned to Constantinople, and his brother Villain was now in command.

108

And the Comans and Wallachians and Greeks pressed them very hard, and wounded many of their horses. Loud were the cries and fierce the onslaught, so that by main force and pure distress they drove the rear-guard back on the battalion of Andrew of Urboise and John of Choisy; and in this manner the Franks retreated, suffering greatly.

The enemy renewed their onslaught so fiercely that they drove the Franks who were nearest to them back on the battalion of Thierri of Tenremonde, the constable. Nor was it long before they drove them back still further on to the battalions led by Charles of the Frêne. And now the Franks had retreated, sore harassed, till they were within half a mile of Rusium. And the others ever pressed upon them more hardily; and the battle went sore against them, and many were wounded, and of their horses. So, as God will suffer misadventures, they could endure no further, but were discomfited; for they were heavily armed, and their enemies lightly; and the latter began to slaughter them.

Alas! well might Christendom rue that day! For of all those six score knights did not more than ten escape who were not killed or taken; and those who escaped came flying into Rusiiim, and rejoined their own people. There was slain Thierri of Tenremonde, the constable, Orri of l'Isle, who was a good knight and highly esteemed, and John of Pompone, Andrew of Urboise, John of Choisy, Guy of Conflans, Charles of the Frêne, Villain the brother of Thierri the seneschal. Nor can this book tell the names of all who were then killed or taken. On that day happened one of the greatest mishaps, and the most grievous that ever befell to the Christendom of the land of Roumania, and one of the most pitiful.

he Comans and Greeks and Wallachians retired, having done according to their will in the land, and won many good horses and good hawberks. And this misadventure happened on the day before the eve of our Lady St. Mary

Candlemas (31st January 1206). And the remnant who had escaped from the discomfiture, together with those who had been in Rusium. escaped from the city, so soon as it was night, and went all night flying, and came on the morrow to the city of Rodosto.

109

NEW INVASION OF JOHANNIZZA; RUIN OF NAPOLI

This dolorous news came to Henry the Regent of the empire, while he was going in procession to the shrine of our Lady of Blachemae, on the day of the feast of our Lady St. Mary Candlemas. And you must know that many were then dismayed in Constantinople, and they thought of a truth that the land was but lost. And Henry, the Regent of the empire, decided that he would place a garrison in Selymbria, which was a two days' journey from Constantinople, and he sent thither Macaire of Sainte-Menehould, with fifty knights to garrison the city.

Now when tidings came to Johannizza, King of Wallachia. as to how his people had fared, he was very greatly rejoiced'; for they had killed or taken a very great part of the best men in the French host. So he sent throughout all his lands to collect as many people as he could, and raised a great host of Comans, and Greeks and Wallachians, and entered into Roumania. And the greater part of the cities held for him, and all the castles; and he had so large a host that it was a marvel.

When the Venetians heard tell that he was coming with so great a force, they abandoned Arcadiopolis. And Johannizza rode with all his hosts till he came to Napoli, which was garrisoned by Greeks and Latins, and belonged to Vemas, who had to wife the empress, the sister of the King of France; and of the Latins was chief Bègue of Fransures, a knight of the land of the Beauvaisais. And Johannizza, the King of Wallachia, caused the city to be assaulted, and took it by force.

There was so great a slaughter of people killed, that it was a marvel. And Bègue of Fransures was taken before Johannizza, who had him killed incontinently, together with all, whether Greek or Latin, who were of any account; and all the meaner folk, and women and children, he caused to, be led away captive to Wallachia. Then did he cause all the city-which was verv good and very rich, and in a good land, to be cast down and utterly destroyed. Thus was the city of Napoli rased to the ground as you have heard.

110

DESTRUCTION OF RODOSTO

Twelve leagues thence lay the city of Rodosto, on the sea. Tt was very strong, and rich, and large, and very well garrisoned by Venetians, And besides all this, there had come thither a body of sergeants, some two thousand strong, and they had also come to guard the city. When they heard that Napoli had been taken by force, and that Johannizza had caused all the people that were therein to be put to death, they fell in to such terror that they were utterly confounded and foredone. As God suffers misadventures to fall upon men, so the Venetians rushed to their ships, helter-skelter, pell-mell, and in such sort that they almost drowned one another; and the mounted sergeants, who came from France and Flanders, and other countries, went flying through the land.

Now listen and hear how little this served them, and what a misadventure was their flight; for the city was so strong, and so well enclosed by good walls and good towers, that no one would ever have ventured to assault it, and that Johannizza had no thought of going thither. But when Johannizza, who was full half a day's journey distant, heard tell that they had fled, he rode thither. The Greeks who had remained in the city, surrendered, and he incontinently caused them to be taken, small and great-save those who escaped-and led captive into Wallachia; and the city he ordered to be destroyed and rased to the ground. Ah! the loss and dar.,iage! for the city was one of the best in Roumania, and of the best situated.

JOHANNIZZA CONTINUES HIS CONQUESTS AND RAVAGES

Near there was another citv called Panedor, which surrendered to him; and he caused it to be utterly destroyed, and the people to be led captive to Wallachia like the people of Rodosto. Afterwards he rode to the city of Heraclea, that lay by a good seaport, and belonged to the Venetians, who had left in it but a weak garrison; so he assaulted it, and took it by force. There aain was a mighty slaughter, and the remnant that escaped the slaughter he caused to be led captive to Wallachia, while the city itself he destroyed, as lie had destroyed the others.

111

Thence he marched to the city of Daonium, which was very strong and fine; and the people did not dare to defend it. So he caused it to be destroyed and rased to the ground. Then he marched to the city of Tzurulum, which had already surrendered to him, and caused it to be destroyed and rased to the ground, and the people to be led away captive. And thus he dealt with every castle and city that surrendered; even though he had promised them safety, he caused the buildings to be destroyed, and the men and women to be led away captive; and no covenant that he made did he ever keep.

Then the Comans and Wallachians scoured the land up to the gates of Constantinople, where Henry the Regent then was, with as many men as he could command; and very dolorous was he and very wroth, because he could not get men enough to defend his land. So the Comans seized the cattle off the land, and took captive men, women, and children, and destroyed the cities and castles, and caused such ruin and desolation that never has man heard tell of greater.

So they came to a city called Athyra, which was twelve leagues from Constantinople, and had been given to Payen of Orléans by Henry, the emperor's brother. This city held a very great number of people, for the dwellers in the country round about had fled thither; and the Comans assaulted it, and took it by force. There the slaughter was so great, that there had been none such in any city where they had been. And you must know that all the castles and all the cities that surrendered to Johannizza under promise of safety were destroyed and rased to the ground, and the people led away captive to Wallachia in such manner as you have heard.

And you must know that within five days' journey from Constantinople there remained nothing to destroy save only the city of Bizye, and the city of Selymbria, which were garrisoned by the French. And in Bizye abode Anseau of Cayeux, with six score knights, and in Salymbria abode Macaire of Sainte-Menehould with fifty knights; and Henry the brother of the Emperor Baldwin remained in Constantinople with the remainder of the host. And you may know that their fortunes were at the lowest, seeing that outside of Constantinople they had kepl& possession of no more than these two cities.

112

THE GREEKS ARE RECONCILED TO THE CRUSADERS - JOHANNIZZA DESIEGES DEMOTICA

When the Greeks who were in the host with Johannizza - the same who had yielded themselves up to him, and rebelled against the Franks - when they saw how he destroyed their castles and cities, and kept no covenant with them, they held themselves to be but dead men, and betrayed. They spoke one to another, and said that as Johannizza had dealt with other cities, so would he deal with Adrianople and Demotica, when he returned thither, and that if these two cities were destroyed, then was Roumania for ever lost.

So they took messengers privily, and sent them to Vernas in Constantinople. And they besought Vernas to cry for pity to Henry, the brother of the Emperor Baldwin, and to the Venetians, so that they might make peace with them; and they themselves, in turn, would restore Adrianople and Demotica to the Franks; and the Greeks would all turn to Henry; and the Greeks and Franks dwell together in good accord.

So a council was held, and many words were spoken this way and that, but in the end it was settled that Adrianople and Demotica, with all their appurtenances, should be bestowed on Vernas and the empress his wife, who was sister to the King Philip of France, and that they should do service therefor to the emperor and to the empire. Such was the convention made and concluded, and so was peace established between the Greeks and the Franks.

Johanizza, the King of Wallachia and Bulgaria, who had sojourned long in Roumania, and wasted the country during the whole of Lent, and for a good while after Easter (2nd April 1206), now retired towards Adrianople and Demotica, and had it in mind to deal with those cities as he had dealt with the other cities of the land. And when the Greeks who were with him saw that he turned towards Adrianople, they began to steal away, both by day and by night, some twenty, thirty, forty, a hundred, at a time.

When he came to Adrianople, he required of those that were within that they should let him enter, as he had entered elsewhere. But they said they would not, and spoke thus: "Sire, when we surrendered to thee, and rebelled against the

113

Franks, thou didst swear to protect us in all good faith, and to keep us in safety. Thou hast not done so, but hast utterly ruined Roumania; and we know full well that thou wilt do unto us as thou hast done unto others." And when Johannizza heard this, he laid siege to Demotica, and erected round it sixteen large petraries, and began to construct engines of every kind for the siege, and to waste all the country round.

Then did those in Adrianople and Demotica take messengers, and send them to Constantinople, to Henry, the Regent of the empire, and to Vemas, and prayed them, for God's sake, to rescue Demotica, which was being besieged. And when those at Constantinople heard these tidings, they decided to succour Demotica. But some there were who did not dare to advise that our people should issue from Constantinople, and so place in jeopardy the few Christian folk that remained. Nevertheless, in the end, as you have heard, it was decided to issue forth, and move on Selymbria.

The cardinal, who was there as legate on the part of the Pope of Rome, preached thereon to the people, and promised a full indulgence to all such as should go forth, and lose their lives on the way. So Henry issued from Constantinople with as many men as he could collect, and marched to the city of Selyrnbria; and he encamped before the city for full eight days. And from day to day came messengers from Adrianople praying him to have mercy upon them, and come to their relief, for if he did not come to their relief, they were but lost.

THE CRUSADERS MARCH TO THE RELIEF OF DEMOTICA

Then did Henry take council with his barons, and their decision was that they would go to the city of Bizve, which was a fair city, and strong. So they did as they had devised, and came to Bizye, and encamped before the city on the eve of the feast of our Lord St. John the Baptist, in June (23rd June 1206). And on the day that they so encamped came messengers from Adrianople, and said to Henry, the brother of the Emperor Baldwin: "Sire, be it known to thee that if thou dost not relieve the city of Demotica, it cannot hold out more than eight days, for Johannizza's petraries have breached the walls in four places, and his men have twice got on to the walls."

114

Then he asked for counsel as to what he should do. Many were the words spoken, to and fro; but in the end they said: " Lord, we have come so far that we shall be for ever shamed if we do not succour Demotica. Let every man now confess and receive the communion; and then let us set our forces in array." And it was reckoned that they had with them about four hundred knights, and of a certainty no more. So they summoned the messengers who had come from Adrianople, and asked them how matters stood, and what number of men Johannizza had with him. And the messengers answered that he had with him at least forty thousand men-at-arms, not reckoning those on foot, of whom they had no count.

Ah God! what a perilous battle-so few against so many 1 In the morning, on the day of the feast of our Lord St. John the Baptist, all confessed and received the communion, and on the following day they marched forward. The van was commanded by Geoffry, the Marshal of Roumania and Champagne, and with him was Macaire of Sainte-Menehould. The second division was under Conon of Béthune and Miles the Brabant; the third under Payen of Orléans and Peter of Bracieux; the fourth was under Anseau of Cayeux; the fifth under Baldwin of Beauvoir; the sixth under Hugh of Beaumetz; the seventh under Henry, brother of the Emperor Baldwin; the eighth, with the Flemings, under Walter of Escornai; Thierri of Loos, who was seneschal, commanded the rear-guard.

So they rode for three days, all in order; nor did any host ever advance seeking battle so perilously. For they were in peril on two accounts; first because they were so few, and those they were about to attack so many; and secondly, because they did not believe the Greeks, with whom they had just made peace, would help them heartily. For they stood in fear lest, when need arose, the Greeks would go over to Johannizza, who, as you have already heard, had been so near to taking Demotica.

JOHANNIZZA RETREATS, FOLLOWED BY THE CRUSADERS

When Johannizza heard that the Franks were coming, he did not dare to abide, but burned his engines of war, and broke up his camp. So he departed from Demotica; and you must know that this was accounted by all the world as a

115

great miracle. And Henry, the Regent of the empire, came on the fourth day (28th June) before Adrianople, and pitched his cainp near the river of Adrianople, in the fairest meadows in the world. When those who were within the city saw his host coming, they issued forth, bearing all their crosses, and in procession, and showed such joy as had never been seen. And well might they rejoice for they had been in evil case.

Then came tidings to the host that Johannizza was lodged at a castle called Rodosto. So in the morning they set forth and marched to those parts to seek battle; and Johannizza broke up his,camp, and marched back towards his own land. The host followed after him for five days, and he as constantly retired before them. On the fifth day they encamped at a very fair and pleasant place by a castle called Fraim; and there they sojoumed three days.

And at this place there was a division in the host, and a company of valiant men separated themselves therefrom because of a quarrel that they had with Henry, the brother of the Emperor Baldwin. Of this company Baldwin of Beauvoir was chief; and Hugh of Beaumetz went with him, and William of Gommegnies and Dreux of Beaurain. There were some fifty knights who departed together in that company; and they never thought the rest would dare to remain in the land in the midst of their enemies.

RENIER OF TRIT RELIEVED AND DELIVERED

Then did Henry, the Regent of the empire, take council with the barons that were with him; and they decided to ride forward. So they rode forward for two days, and encamped in a very fair valley, near a castle called Moniac. The castle yielded itself to them, and they remained there five days; and then said they would go and relieve Renier of Trit, who was besieged in Stanimac, and had been shut up therein for thirteen months. So Henry the Regent of the empire, remained in the camp, with a great part of the host, and the remainder went forward to relieve Renier of Trit at Stanimac.

And you must know that those who went forward went in very great peril, and that any rescue so full of danger has but seldom been undertaken, seeing that they rode for three days through the land of their enemies. In this rescue took part

116

Conon of Béthune, and Geoffry of Villehardouin, Marshal of Roumania and Champagne, and Macaire of Sainte-Menehould, and Miles the Brabant, and Peter of Bracieux, and Payen of Orléans, and Anseau of Cayeux, and Thierri of Loos, and William of Perchoi, and a body of Venetians under command of Andrew Valère. So they rode forward till they came to the castle of Stanimac, and approached so near that they could now see it.

Renier of Trit was on the walls, and he perceived the advanced guard, which was under Geoffry the Marshal, and the other battalions, approaching in very good order; and he knew not what people they might be. And no wonder that he was in doubt, for of a long time he had heard no tidings of us ; and he thought we were Greeks coming to besiege him.

Geoffry the Marshal of Roumania and Champagne took certain Turcoples *[soldiers born of a Turkish father atid a Greek mother]* and mounted cross-bowmen and sent them forward to see if they could learn the condition of the castle; for they knew not if those within it were alive or dead, seeing that of a long time they had heard no tidings of them. And when these came before the castle, Renier of Trit and his men knew them; and you may well think what joy they had l They issued forth and came to meet their friends, and all made great joy of each other.

The barons quartered themselves in a very good city that lay at the foot of the castle, and had aforetime besieged the castle. Then said the barons that they had often heard tell that the Emperor Baldwin had died in Johannizza's prison, but that they did not believe it. Renier of Trit, however, told them of a truth that the emperor was dead, and then they believed it. Greatly did many then grieve; alas I if only their grief had not been beyond remedy I

So they lay that night in the city; and on the morrow they departed, and abandoned Stanimac. They rode for two days., and on the third they came to the camp, below the castle of Moniac, that lies on the river Arta, where Henry, the Emperor's brother, was waiting for them. Greatly did those of the host rejoice over Renier of Trit, who had thus been rescued from durance, and great was the credit given to those who had brought him back, for they had gone for him in great peril.

117

HENRY CROWNED EMPEROR - JOHANNIZZA RAVAGES THE COUNTRY AGAIN - THE EMPEROR MARCHES AGAINST HIM

The barons now resolved that they would go to Constantinople, and crown Henry, the brother of the Emperor Baldwin as emperor, and leave in the country Vemas, and all the Greeks of the land, together with forty knights, whom Henry, the Regent of the empire, would leave with him. So Henry, the Regent of the empire, and the other barons, went towards Constantinople, and they rode from day to day till they came thither, and right well were they received. They crowned Henry as emperor with great joy and great honour in the church of St. Sophia, on the Sunday (20th August) after the festival of our Lady St. Mary, in August. And this was in the year of the Incarnation of our Lord Jesus Christ twelve hundred and six.

Now when Johannizza, the King of Wallachia and Bulgaria, heard that the emperor had been crowned in Constantinople, and that Vemas had remained in the land of Adrianople and Demotica, he collected together as large a force as he could. And Vemas had not rebuilt the walls of Demotica where they had been breached by Johannizza with his petraries and mangonels, and he had set but a weak garrison therein. So Johannizza marched on Demotica, and took it, and destroyed it, and rased the walls to the ground, and overran the whole country, and took men, women, and children for a prey, and wrought devastation. Then did those in Adrianople beseech the Emperor Henry to succour them, seeing that Demotica had been lost in such cruel sort.

Then did the Emperor Henry summon as many people as he could, and issued from Constantinople, and rode day by day towards Adrianople, with all his forces in order. And Johannizza, the King of Wallachia, who was in the land, when he heard that the emperor was coming, drew back into his own land. And the Emperor Henry rode forward till he came to Adrianople, and he encamped outside the city in a meadow.

Then came the Greeks of the land, and told him that johanriizza, the King of Wallachia, was carrying off men and women and cattle, and that he had destroyed Demotica, and wasted the country round; and that he was still within a

day's march. The emperor settled that he would follow after, and do battle-if so be that Johannizza would abide his coming-and deliver the men and women who were being led away captive. So he rode after Johannizza, and Johannizza retired as the emperor advanced, and the emperor followed him for four days. Then they came to a city called Veroi.

When those who were in the city saw the host of the Emperor Henry approaching, they fled into the mountains and abandoned the city. And the emperor came with all his host, and encamped before the city, and found it well furnished with corn and meat, and such other things as were needful. So they sojourned there for two days, and the emperor caused his men to overrun the surrounding country, and they obtained a large booty in beeves and cows and buffaloes, and otl-ler beasts in very great plenty. Then he departed from Veroi with all his booty, and rode to another city, a day's journey distant, called Blisnon. And as the other Greeks had abandoned Veroi, so did the dwellers in Blisnon abandon their city; and he found it furnished with all things necessary, and quartered himself there.

THE EMPEROR MEETS JOHANNIZZA, AND RECAPTURES HIS PRISONERS

Then came tidings that in a certain valley, three leagues distant from the host, were the men and women whom ohannizza was leading away captive, together with 9.11 his plunder, and all his chariots. Then did Henry appoint that the Greeks from Adrianople and Demotica should go and recover the captives and the plunder, two battalions of knights going with them; and as had been arranged, so was this done on the morrow. The command of the one battalion was given to Eustace, the brother of the Emperor Henry of Constantinople, and the command of the other to Macaire of Sainte-Menehould.

So they rode, they and the Greeks, till they came to the valley of which they had been told; and there they found the captives. And Johannizza's men engaged the Emperor Henry's men, and men and horses were killed and wounded On either side; but by the goodness of God, the Franks had

the advantage, and rescued the captives, and caused them to turn again, and brought them away.

And you must know that this was a mighty deliverance; for the captives numbered full twenty thousand men, women, and children; and there were full three thousand chariots laden with their clothes and baggage, to say nothing of other booty in good quantity. The line of the captives, as they came to the camp, was two great leagues in length, and they reached the camp that night. Then was the Emperor Henry greatly rejoiced, and all the other barons; and they had the captives lodged apart, and well guarded, with their goods, so that they lost not one pennyworth of what they possessed. On the morrow the Emperor Henry rested for the sake of the people he had delivered. And on the day after he left that country, and rode day by day till he came to Adrianople.

There he set free the men and women he had rescued; and each one went whithersoever he listed, to the land where he was born, or to any other place. The booty, of which he had great plenty, was divided in due shares among the host. So the Emperor Henry sojourned there five days, and then rode to the city of Demotica, to see how far it had been destroyed, and whether it could again be fortified. He encamped before the city, and saw, both he and his barons, that in the state in which it then was, it were not well to refortify it.

PROJECTED MARRIAGE BETWEEN THE EMPEROR AND THE DAUGHTER OF BONIFACE - THE CRUSADERS RAVAGE THE LANDS OF JOHANNIZZA

Then came to the camp, as envoy, a baron, Otho of La Roche by name, belonging to the Marquis Boniface of Montferrat. He came to speak of a marriage that had been spoken of aforetime between the daughter of Boniface, the Marquis of Montferrat, and the Emperor Henry; and brought tidings that the lady had come from Lombardy, whence her father had sent to summon her, and that she was now at Salonika. Then did the emperor take council, and it was decided that the marriage should be ratified on either side. So the envoy, Otho of La Roche, returned to Salonika.

The emperor had reassembled his men, who had gone to place in safe holding the booty taken at Veroi. And he marched day by day from Adrianople till he came to the land

120

of Johannizza, the King of Wallachia and Bulgaria. They came to a city called Ferme, and took it, and entered in, and won much booty. They remained there for three days, and overran all the land, got very much spoil, and destroyed a city called Aquilo.

On the fourth day they departed from Ferme, which was a city fair and well situated, with hot water springs for bathing, the finest in the world; and the emperor caused the city to be burned and destroyed, and they carried away much spoil, in cattle and goods. Then they rode day by day till they came back to the city of Adrianople; and they sojourned in the land till the feast of All Saints (1st November 1206), when they could no longer carry on the war because of the winter. So Henry and all his barons, who were much aweary of campaigning, turned their faces towards Constantinople; and he left at Adrianople, among the Greeks, a man of his named Peter of Radinghem, with ten knights.

THE EMPEROR RESUMES THE WAR AGAINST THEODORE LASCARIS

At that time Theodore Lascaris, who held the land on the other side of the straits towards Turkey, was at truce with the Emperor Henry; but that truce he had not kept well, having broken and violated it. So the emperor held council, and sent to the other side of the straits, to the city of Piga, Peter of Bracieux, to whom land had been assigned in those parts, and with him Payen of Orléans, and Anseau of Cayeux, and Eustace, the emperor's brother, and a great part of his best men to the number of seven score knights. These began to make war in very grim and earnest fashion against Theodore Lascaris, and greatly wasted his land.

They marched to a land called Skiza, which was surrounded by the sea except on one side. And in old days the way of entry had been defended with walls and towers, and moats, but these were now decayed. So the host of the French entered in, and Peter of Bracieux, to whom the land had been devised, began to restore the defences, and built two castles, and made two fortified ways of entry. From thence they overran the land of Lascaris, and gained much booty and cattle, and brought such booty and cattle into their island: Theodore Lascaris, on the other hand, harked back upon

121

Skiza, so that there were frequent battles and skirmishes, and losses on the one side and on the other; and the war in those parts was fierce and perilous.

Now let us leave speaking of those who were at Skiza, and speak of Thierri of Loos, who was seneschal, and to whom Nicomedia should have belonged; and Nicomedia lay a day's journey from Nice the Great, the capital of the land of Theodore Lascaris. Thierri then went thither, with a great body of the emperor's men, and found that the castle had been destroyed. So he enclosed and fortified the church of St. Sophia, which was very large and fair, and maintained the war in that place.

ADVANTAGES OBTAINED BY BONIFACE - MARRIAGE OF HIS DAUGHTER WITH THE EMPEROR

At that time the Marquis Boniface of Montferrat departed from Salonika, and went to Seres, which Johannizza had destroyed; and he rebuilt it; and afterwards rebuilt a castle called Drama in the valley of Philippi. All the country round about surrendered to him, and came under his rule; and he wintered in the land.

Meanwhile, so much time had gone by, that Christmas was now past. Then came messengers from the marquis to the emperor at Constantinople to say that the marquis had sent his daughter in a galley to the city of Abydos. So the Emperor Henry sent Geoffry the Marshal of Roumania and Champagne, and Miles the Brabant, to bring the lady; and these rode day by day till they came to Abydos.

They found the lady, who was very good and fair, and saluted her on behalf of their lord Henry, the emperor, and brought her to Constantinople in great honour. So the Emperor Henry was wedded to her in the Church of St. Sophia, on the Sunday after the feast of our Lady St. Mary Candlemas (4th February 1207), with great joy and in great pomp; and they both wore a crown; and high were the marriage-feastings in the palace of Bucoleon. Thus, as you have just heard, was the marriage celebrated between the emperor and the daughter of the Marquis Boniface, Agnes the empress by name.

THEODORE LASCARIS FORMS AN ALLIANCE WITH JOHANNIZZA

Theodore Lascaris, who was warring against the Emperor Henry, took messengers and sent them to Johannizza, the King of Wallachia and Bulgaria. And he advised Johannizza that all the forces of the Emperor Henry were fighting against him (Lascaris) on the other side of the straits towards Turkey; that the emperor was in Constantinople with but very few people; and that now was the time for vengeance, inasmuch as he himself would be attacking the emperor on the one side, and Johannizza on the other, and the emperor had so few men that he would not be able to defend himself against both. Now Johannizza had already engaged a great host of Comans, who were on their way to join his host; and had collected together as large a force of Wallachians and Bulgarians as ever he could. And so much time had now gone by, that it was the beginning of Lent (7th March 1207).

Macaire of Sainte-Menehould had begun to build a castle at Charax, which lies on a gulf of the sea, six leagues from Nicomedia, towards Constantinople.

And William of Sains began to build another castle at Cibotos, that lies on the gulf of Nicomedia, on the other side, towards Nice. And you must know that the Emperor Henry had as much as he could do near Constantinople; as also the barons who were in the land. And well does Geoffry of Villehardouin, the Marshal of Champagne and Roumania, who is dictating this work, bear witness, that never at any time were people so distracted and oppressed by war; this was by reason that the host were scattered in so many places.

SIEGE OF ADRIANOPLE BY JOHANNIZZA - SIEGE OF SKIZA AND CIBOTOS BY LASCARIS

Then Johannizza left Wallachia with all his hosts, and with a great host of Comans who joined themselves to him, and entered Roumania. And the Comans overran the country up to the gates of Constantinople; and he himself besieged Adrianople, and erected there thirty-three great petraries, which hurled stones against the walls and the towers. And inside Adrianople were only the Greeks and

123

Peter of Radinghem, who had been set there by the emperor, with ten knights. Then the Greeks and the Latins together sent to tell the Emperor Henry how Johannizza had besieged them, and prayed for succour.

Much was the emperor distraught when he heard this; for his forces on the other side of the straits were so scattered, and were everywhere so hard pressed that they could do no more than they were doing, while he himself had but few men in Constantinople. None the less he undertook to take the field with as many men as he could collect, in the Easter fortnight; and he sent word to Skiza, where most of his people were, that they should come to him. So these began to come to him by sea; Eustace, the brother of the Emperor Henry, and Anseau of Cayeux, and the main part of their men, and thus only Peter of Bracieux, and Payen of Orléans, with but few men, remained in Skiza.

When Theodore Lascaris heard tidings that Adrianople was besieged, and that the Emperor Henry, through utter need, was recalling his people, and did not know which way to tum-whether to this side or to that-so heavily was he oppressed by the war, then did Lascaris with the greater zeal gather together all the people he could,, and pitched his tents and pavilions before the gates of Skiza; and many were the battles fought before Skiza, some lost and some won. And when Theodore Lascaris saw that there were few people remaining in the city, he took a great part of his host, and such ships as he could collect on the sea, and sent them to the castle of Cibotos, which William of Sains was fortifying; and they set siege to the castle by sea and land, on the Saturday in mid-Lent (31st March 1207).

Within were forty knights, very good men, and Macaire of Sainte-Menehould was their chief; and their castle was as yet but little fortified, so that their foes could come at them with swords and lances. The enemy attacked them by land and by sea very fiercely; and the assault lasted during the whole of Saturday, and our people defended themselves very well. And this book bears witness that never did fifty knights defend themselves at greater disadvantage against such odds. And well may this appear, for of the knights that were there, all were wounded save five only; and one was killed, who was nephew to Miles the Brabant, and his name was Giles.

124

THE EMPEROR ATTACKS THE FLEET OF THEODORE LASCARIS, AND RESCUES CIBOTOS

Before this assault began, on the Saturday morning, there came a messenger flying to Constantinople. He found the Emperor Henry in the palace of Blachernae, sitting at meat, and spoke to him thus: "Sire, be it known to you that those at Cibotos are being attacked by land and sea; and if you do not speedily deliver them, they will be taken, and but dead men."

With the emperor were Conon of Béthune, and Geoffry the Marshal of Champagne, and Miles the Brabant, and but very few people. And they held a council, and the council was but short, and the emperor went down to the shore, and entered into a galleon; and each one was to take ship such as he could find. And it was proclaimed throughout the city that all were to follow the emperor in the utter need wherein he stood, to go and rescue his men, seeing that without help they were but lost. Then might you have seen the whole city of Constantinople all a-swarm with Venetians and Pisans and other seafaring folk, running to their ships, helterskelter and pell-mell; and with them entered into the ships the knights, fully armed; and whosoever was first ready, he first left port to go after the emperor.

So they went rowing hard all the evening, as long as the light lasted, and all through the night till the dawn of the following day. And the emperor had used such diligence, that a little after sun-rising he came in sight of Cibotos, and of the host surrounding it by sea and land. And those who were within the castle had not slept that night, but had kept guard through the whole night, however sick or wounded they might be, as men who expected nothing but death.

The emperor saw that the Greeks were close to the walls and about to assault the city. Now he himself had but few of his people with him-among them were Geoffry the Marshal in another ship, and Miles the Brabant, and certain Pisans, and other knights, so that he had some sixteen ships great and small, while on the other side there were full sixty. Nevertheless they saw that if they waited for their people, and suffered the Greeks to assault Cibotos, then those within

125

must be all killed or taken; and when they saw this they decided to sail against the enemy's ships.

They sailed thitherward therefore in line; and all those on board the ships were fully armed, and with their helms laced. And when the Greeks, who were about to attack the castle, saw us coming, they perceived that help was at hand for the besieged, and they avoided the castle, and came to meet us; and all this great host, both horse and foot, drew up on the shore. And the Greeks on ship-board *[The meaning here is a little obscure in the original]* when they saw that the emperor and his people meant to attack them in any case, drew back towards those on shore, so that the latter might give them help with bows and darts.

So the emperor held them close with his seventeen ships, till the shouts of those coming from Constantinople began to reach him; and when the night fell so many had come up that the Franks were everywhere in force upon the sea; and they lay all armed during the night, and cast anchor. And they settled that as soon as they saw the day, they would go and do battle with the enemy on the shore, and also seize their ships. But when it came to about midnight, the Greeks dragged all their ships to land, and set fire to them, and burned them all, and broke up their camp, and went away flying.

The Emperor Henry and his host were right glad of the victory that God had given them,,and that they had thus been able to succour their people. And when it came to be morning, the emperor and his barons went to the castle of Cibotos, and found those who were therein very sick, and for the most part sore wounded. And the emperor and his people looked at the castle, and saw that it was so weak as not to be worth the holding. So they gathered all their people into the ships, and left the castle and abandoned it. Thus did the Emperor Henry return to Constantinople.

JOHANNIZZA RAISES THE SIEGE OF ADRIANOPLE

Johannizza, the king of Wallachia, who had besieged Adrianople, gave himself no rest, for his petraries, of which he had many, cast stones night and day against the walls and towers, and damaed the walls and towers very greatly. And he set his sappers to mine the walls, and made many

126

assaults. And well did those who were within, both Greeks and Latins, maintain themselves, and often did they beg the Emperor Henry to succour them, and wam him that, if he did not succour them, they were utterly undone. The emperor was much distraught; for when he wished to go and succour his people at Adrianople on the one side, then Theodore Lascaris pressed upon him so straitly on the other side, that of necessity he was forced to draw back.

So Johannizza remained during the whole month of April (1207) before Adrianople; and he came so near to taking it that in two places he beat down the walls and towers to the ground, and his men fought hand to hand, with swords and lances, against those who were within. Also he made assaults in force, and the besieged defended themselves well; and there were many killed and wounded on one side and on the other.

As it pleases God that adventures should be ordered, so it befell that the Comans who had overrun the land, and gained much booty, and returned to the camp before Adrianople, with all their spoils, now said they would remain with Johannizza no longer, but go back to their own land. Thus the Comans abandoned Johannizza. And without them he dared not remain before Adrianople. So he departed from before the city, and left it.

And you must know that this was held to be a great miracle: that the siege of a city so near to the taking should be abandoned, and by a man possessed of such power. But as God wills, so do events befall. Those in Adrianople made no delay in begging the emperor, for the love of God, to come to them as soon as he could; for sooth it was that if Johannizza, the King of Wallachia returned, they would all be killed or taken.

SKIZA AGAIN BESIEGED BY THEODORE LASCARIS - THE EMPEROR DELIVERS THE CITY

The emperor, with as many men as he possessed, had prepared to go to Adrianople, when tidings came, very grievous, that Escurion, who was admiral of the galleys of Theodore Lascaris, had entered with seventeen galleys into the straits of Abydos, in the channel of St. George, and come before Skiza, where Peter of Bracieux then was, and Payen of

Orléans; and that the said Escurion was besieging the city by sea, while Theodore Lascaris was besieging it by land. Moreover, the people of the land of Skiza had rebelled against Peter of Bracieux, as also those of Marmora, and had wrought him great harm, and killed many of his people.

When these tidi . ngs came to Constantinople, they were greatly dismayed. Then did the Emperor Henry take council with his men, and his barons, and the Venetians also; and they said that if they did not succour Peter of Bracieux, and Payen of Orléans, they were but dead men, and the land would be lost. So they armed fourteen galleys in all diligence, and set in them the Venetians of most note, and all the barons of the emperor.

In one galley entered Conon of Béthune and his people; in another Geoffry of Villehardouin and his people; in the third Macaire of Sainte-Menehould and his people; in the fourth Miles the Brabant in the fifth Anscau of Cayeux; in the sixth Thierri of Loos, who was seneschal of Roumania; m the seventh William of Perchoi; and in the eighth Eustace the Emperor's brother. Thus did the Emperor Henry put into all these galleys the best people that he had; and when they left the port of Constantinople, well did all say that never had galleys been better armed, nor manned with better men. And thus, for this time, the march on Adrianople was again put off.

Those who were in the galleys sailed down the straits, right towards Skiza. How Escurion, the admiral of Theodore Lascaris' galleys, heard of it, I know not; but he abandoned Skiza, and went away, and fled down the straits. And the others chased him two days and two nights, beyond the straits of Abydos, forty miles. And when they saw they could not come up with him, they turned back, and came to Skiza, and found there Peter of Bracieux and Payen of Orléans; and Theodore Lascaris had dislodged from before the city and repaired to his own land. Thus was Skiza relieved, as you have just heard; and those in the galleys turned back to Constantinople, and prepared once more to march on Adrianople.

THE EMPEROR TWICE DELIVERS NICOMEDIA, BESIEGED BY THEODORE LASCARIS

Theodore Lascaris sent the most part of his force into the land of Nicomedia. And the people of Thierri of Loos, who had fortified the church of St. Sophia, and were therein, besought their lord and the emperor to come to their relief; for if they received no help they could not hold out, especially as they had no provisions. Through sheer distress and sore need, the Emperor Henry and his people agreed that they must once more abandon thought of going to Adrianople, and cross the straits of St. George, to the Turkish side, with as many people as they could collect, and succour Nicomedia.

And when the people of Theodore Lascaris heard that the emperor was coming, they avoided the land, and retreated towards Nice the Great. And when the emperor knew of it, he took council, and it was decided that Thierri of Loos, the seneschal of Roumania, should abide in Nicomedia, with all his knights, and all his sergeants, to guard the land; and Macaire of Sainte-Menehould should abide at Charax, and William of Perchoi in Skiza; and each defend the land where he abode.

Then did the Emperor Henry, and the remainder of his people return to Constantinople, and prepare once again to go towards Adrianople. And while he was so preparing, Thierri of Loos the seneschal, who was in Nicomedia, and William of Perchoi, and all their people, went out foraging on a certain day. And the people of Theodore Lascaris knew of it, and surprised them, and fell upon them. Now the people of Theodore Lascaris were very many, and our people very few. So the battle began, and they fought hand to hand, and before very long the few were not able to stand against the many.

Thierri of Loos did right well, as also his people; he was twice struck down, and by main strength his men remounted him. And William of Perchoi was also struck down, and remounted and rescued. But numbers hemmed them in too sore, and the Franks were discomfited. There was taken Thierri of Loos, wounded in the face, and in peril of death. There, too, were most of his people taken, for few escaped. William of Perchoi fled on a hackney, wounded in the hand.

129

Those that escaped from the discomfiture rallied in the church of St. Sophia.

He who dictates this history heard blame attached in this affair-whether rightly or wrongly he knows not-to a certain knight named Anseau of Remi, who was liegeman of Thierri of Loos the seneschal, and chief of his men; and who abandoned him in the fray.

Then did those who had returned to the church of St. Sophia in Nicomedia, viz. William of Perchoi and Anseau of Remi, take a messenger, and send him flying to Constantinople, to the Emperor Henry; and they told the emperor what had befallen, how the seneschal had been taken with his men; how they themselves were besieged in the church of St. Sophia, in Nicomedia, and how they had food for no more than five days; and they told him he must know of a certainty that if he did not succour them they must be killed or taken. The emperor, as one hearing a cry of distress, passed over the straits of St. George, he and his people, each as best he could, and pell-mell, to go to the relief of those in Nicomedia. And so the march to Adrianople was put off once more.

When the emperor had passed over the straits of St. George, he set his troops in array, and rode day by day till he came to Nicomedia. When the people of Theodore Lascaris, and his brothers, who formed the host, heard thereof, they drew back, and passed over the mountain on the other side, towards Nice. And the emperor encamped by Nicomedia in a very fair field that lay beside the river on this side of the mountain. He had his tents and pavilions pitched; and caused his men to overrun and harry the land, because the people had rebelled when they heard that Thierri of Loos, the seneschal, was taken; and the emperor's men captured much cattle and many prisoners.

TRUCE WITH THEODORE LASCARIS - THE EMPEROR INVADES THE LANDS OF JOHANNIZZA

The Emperor Henry sojourned after this manner for five days in the meadow by Nicomedia. And while he was thus sojourning, Theodore Lascaris took messengers, and sent them to him, asking him to make a truce for two years, on condition that the emperor would suffer him to demolish

130

Skiza and the fortress of the church of St. Sophia of Nicomedia, while he, on his side, would yield up all the prisoners taken in the last victory, or at other times of whom he had a great many in his land.

Now the emperor took council with his people; and they said that they could not maintain two wars at the same time, and that it was better to suffer loss as proposed than suffer the loss of Adrianople, and the land on the other side of the straits; and moreover that they.would (by agreeing to this truce) cause division between their enemies, viz. Johannizza, the King of Wallachia and Bulgaria and Theodore Lascaris who were now friends, and helped one another in the war.

The matter was thus settled and agreed to. Then the Emperor Henry summoned Peter of Bracieux from Skiza; and he came to him; and the Emperor Henry so wrought with him that he gave up Skiza into his hands, and the emperor delivered it to Theodore Lascaris to be demolished, as also the church of St. Sophia of Nicomedia. So was the truce established, and so were the fortresses demolished. Thierri of Loos was given up, and all the other prisoners.

Then the Emperor Henry repaired to Constantinople, and undertook once more to go to Adrianople with as many men as he could collect. He assembled his host at Selymbria; and so much time had already passed that this did not take place till after the feast of St. John, in June (1207). And he rode day by day till he came to Adrianople, and encamped in the fields before the city. And those within the city, who had greatly desired his coming, went out to meet him in procession, and received him very gladly.. And all the Greeks of the land came with them.

The emperor remained only one day before the city to see all the damage that Johannizza had done to the walls and towers, with mines and petraries; and these had worked great havoc to the city. And on the morrow he departed', and marched towards the country of Johannizza, and so marched for four days. On the fifth day he came to the foot of the mountain of Wallachia, to a city called Euloi, which Johannizza had newly repeopled with his folk. And when the people of the land saw the host coming, they abandoned the city, and fled into the mountains.

131

THE E MPEROR'S FORAGERS SUFFER LOSS

The Emperor Henry and the host of the French encamped before the city; and the foraging parties overran the land and captured oxen, and cows, and beeves in great plenty and other beasts. And those from Adrianople, who had brought their chariots with them, and were poor and illfurnished with food, loaded their chariots with corn and other grain; and they found also provisions in plenty and loaded with them, in great quantities, the other chariots that they had captured. So the host sojourned there for three days; and every day the foraging parties went foraging throughout the land; but the land was full of mountains, and strong defiles, and the host lost many foragers, who adventured themselves madly.

In the end, the Emperor Henry sent Anscau of Cayeux to guard the foragers, and Eustace his brother, and Thierri of Flanders, his nephew, and Walter of Escomai, and John Bliaud. Their four battalions went to guard the foragers, and entered into a land rough and mountainous. And when their people had overrun the land, and wished to return, they found the defiles very well guarded. For the Wallachians of the country had assembled, and fought against them, and did them great hurt, both to men and horses. Hardly were our men put to it to escape discomfiture; and the knights had, of necessity, to dismount and go on foot. But by God's help they returned to the camp, though not without great loss and damage.

On the morrow the Emperor Henry, and the host of the French departed thence, and marched day by day till they came to Adrianople; and they stored therein the corn and other provisions that they brought with them. The emperor sojourned in the field before the city some fifteen days.

HOMAGE RENDERED BY BONIFACE TO THE EMPEROR, AND BY GEOFFRY OF VILLEHARDOUIN TO BONIFACE

At that time Boniface, the Marquis of Montferrat, who was at Seres, which he had fortified, rode forth as far as Messinopolis, and all the land surrendered to his will. Then he took messengers, and sent them to the Emperor Henry, and told him that he would right willingly speak with him

132

by the river that runs below Cypsela. Now they two had never been able to speak together face to face since the conquest of the land, for so many enemies lay between them that the one had never been able to come to the other. And when the emperor and those of his councilheardthat themarquis Boniface was at Messinopolis, they rejoiced greatly; and the emperor sent back word by the messengers that he would speak with the marquis on the day appointed.

So the emperor went thitherward, and he left Conon of Bethune to guard the land near Adrianople, with one hundred knights. And they came on the set day to the place of meeting in a very fair field, near the city of Cypsela. The emperor came from one side, and the marquis from the other, and they met with very great joy; nor is that to be wondered at, seeing they had not, of a long time, beheld one another. And the marquis asked the emperor for tidings of his daughter Agnes; and the emperor told him she was with child, and the marquis was glad thereof and rejoiced. Then did the marquis become liegeman to the emperor, and held from him his land, as he had done from the Emperor Baldwin, his brother. And the marquis gave to Geoffry of Villehardouin, Marshal of Roumania and Champagne, the city of Messinopolis, and all its appurtenances, or else that of Seres, whichever he liked best; and the Marshal became his liegeman, save in so far as he owed fealty to the emperor of Constantinople.

They sojourned thus in that field for two days, in great joy, and said that, as God had granted that they should come together, so might they yet again defeat their enemies. And they made agreement to meet at the end of the summer, in the month of October, with all their forces, in the meadow before the city of Adrianople, and make war against the King of Wallachia. So they separated joyous and well content. The marquis went to Messinopolis, and the Emperor Henry towards Constantinople.

BONIFACE IS KILLED IN A BATTLE AGAINST THE BULGARIANS

When the marquis had come to Messinopolis, he did not remain there more than five days before he rode forth, by the advice of the Greeks of the land, on an expedition to the mountain of Messinopolis, which was distant a long day's

133

journey. And when he had been through the land, and was about to depart, the Bulgarians of the land collected and saw that the marquis had but a small force with him. So they came from all parts and attacked the rear-guard. And when the marquis heard the shouting, he leapt on a horse, all unarmed as he was, with a lance in his hand. And when he came together, where the Bulgarians were fighting with the rear-guard, hand to hand, he ran in upon them, and drove them a great way back.

Then was the Marquis Boniface of Montferrat wounded with an arrow, in the thick of the arm, beneath the shoulder, mortally, and he began to lose blood. And when his men saw it, they began to be dismayed, and to lose heart, and to bear themselves badly. Those who were round the marquis held him up, and he was losing much blood; and he began to faint. And when his men perceived that he could give them no farther help, they were the more dismayed, and began to desert him. So were they discomfited by misadventure; and those who remained by him-and they were but few-were killed.

The head of the Marquis Boniface of Montferrat was cut off, and the people of the land sent it to Johannizza; and that was one of the greatest joys that ever Johannizza had. Alas! what a dolorous mishap for the Emperor Henry, and for all the Latins of the land of Roumania, to lose such a man by such a misadventure-one of the best barons and most liberal, and one of the best knights in the world! And this misadventure befell in the year of the Incarnation of Jesus Christ, twelve hundred and seven.

END

www.ingramcontent.com/pod-product-compliance
Lightning Source LLC
Chambersburg PA
CBHW022011050726
47499CB00007BA/2261